Kids @ the Crossroads

Aztec

by Laura Scandiffio
art by Tina Holdcroft

annick press   toronto + new york + vancouver

Note to Readers

"Aztec" is the name we now use for the people who ruled most of Mexico before the arrival of the Spanish in the 1500s. But the Aztecs called themselves "Mexica." The name "Aztec" comes from "Aztlan," the ancient homeland of the Mexica described in their own histories. Whether Aztlan existed or not is uncertain, but the Mexica did leave the north of Mexico and travel south to the Valley of Mexico, where they founded their great capital Tenochtitlan and built an empire through conquest.

Pronouncing Mexica words

The language of the Mexica was Nahuatl (still spoken in parts of Mexico today). Some Nahuatl words made their way into Spanish, and from there into many languages, including English: *tomato*, *chocolate*, *coyote*, and *avocado* are a few examples.

In almost all Nahuatl words, stress is placed on the second-last syllable. The letter *x* is pronounced "sh" and *z* is pronounced "s." Here is a sample of words and how to say them:

calmecac (school for nobles and priests) cal-MEH-cac
Huitzilopochtli (patron god of the Mexica) wee-tsee-loh-POCH-tlee
Mexica meh-SHEE-kah
Motecuhzoma (emperor of the Mexica) moh-teh-koo-SOH-ma
Quetzalcoatl (patron god of priests) keht-sahl-COH-atl
Tenochtitlan (capital city) teh-noch-TEE-tlan
Tezcatlipoca (patron god of warriors, rulers) tehs-cah-tlee-POH-cah
Texcoco (name of a city and lake) tesh-CO-co
Tlaxcalla (a kingdom, enemy of the Mexica) tlash-CAH-lah

About Me

Name:
Yoatl. (It sounds like "YOH-atl" and it means "war." Lots of boys have the same name.) This is me.

Age:
12

Home:
City of Tenochtitlan, in the center of the world.

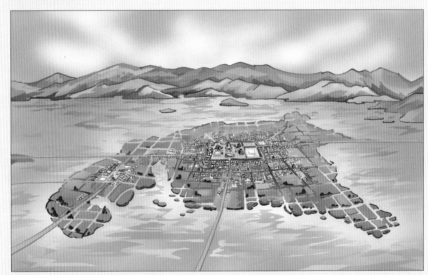

This is my house.

Future job:
That's the problem, everything's changed now.

Brothers and sisters:
One sister, Tepin, 14

Things I can do:
Guess riddles. Name most of the gods and their feast days.
Make rhymes.

Things I'd like to do:
Interpret dreams. Read the stars like my sister is learning to do.
Drink cocoa someday, like the very rich people.

Favorite food:
The maize-cakes my mother makes

Favorite color:
Turquoise, the color of the most beautiful stone and also, I'm told,
the color of the Great Sea

Person I most admire:
My father, of course

Most prized possessions:
An amulet my mother says I can have when I'm older, as long as I don't
show it to anyone. The bright green quetzal feather my father brought
home from the Hot Lands; it changes color when you turn it.

Turquoise

Quetzal

1st day of Tozoztontli   1 of 3

THE MEXICA CALENDAR

The priests understand our complex calendars,
but the rest of us who need to count the
days can get by with a little knowledge:

We have two calendars, one sacred, the
other a solar calendar for keeping track of
the seasons and days. The year has 18 months,
each 20 days long. That leaves five leftover
days, which are so unlucky nobody does anything during them. Those born during that
time spend their lives making offerings to the
gods to change their terrible fate. The years
are counted in a 52-year cycle; we keep track

▶

1st day of Tozoztontli (small vigil), year 1 Reed
Fallen Idol

Today I felt something new. How do I describe it? It's as if I've plunged
from a high, sunny, and safe place down into somewhere cold and dark
where nothing is certain. I think this feeling must be what shame is.
Shame, and maybe fear too.

This morning was ordinary. After I sprinkled seeds and fed the
turkey in our courtyard garden, I spent the morning wandering alongside the canal, following the canoes as they came and went. My sister
and I used to try to race them when we were small. Once the sun
climbed higher, I headed home to escape the heat, and there he was.
It took a moment for my eyes to get used to the shady room, so at first
I didn't know him, sitting on the floor with his back to me. My heart
jumped when I recognized the broad shoulders and creased neck.

by pairing a number from 1 to 13 with one of four names. Right now the year is 1 Reed.

Each month has its own rituals, and honors a different god with feasting, celebrating, and sacrifice. Here are a few:

Uey tozoztli (Great Vigil): Feasts to honor the god and goddess of maize.

Toxcatl, the feast of Tezcatlipoca, the most powerful god: A young man, after living like a lord for a year, is sacrificed.

Etzalqualiztli (Eating of Porridge): Warriors pound on people's doors demanding porridge or else they'll knock down their walls. Jewels and hearts are offered to Tlaloc, the rain god, and to the lake.

Uey tecuilhuitl (Great Feast Day of the Lords): Food is handed out to all commoners. Warriors sing, dance, and feast; women dance.

Reed

It was my father, returned suddenly from his mission. Across from him, my mother, usually so quiet, was chattering the way she does when she is happiest. And next to her, cross-legged on the ground, was my sister, Tepin. I was surprised to see her home from the temple school.

Tepin helped my mother make a hasty meal of maize porridge and beans over the hearth. For a while it felt like our old life again, when Tepin was home and made me laugh and we were together all the time. But the good mood didn't last. Soon my mother and father were talking in hushed tones. Tepin noticed too; we looked at each other, but said nothing.

That's when they came in. A war commander I'd never seen before, with two high-ranking warriors, intimidating in all their feathers and gold. My father stood up at once and faced them. They were haughty-looking. My mother offered them bowls of food, but the commander refused with a wave of his hand. None of them sat down to join us.

They spoke to my father about his recent mission—how he and other trusted warriors had been sent to teach obedience to the people of Cuetlaxtlan, who had stopped paying tribute to our emperor. I knew that already. But now the commander said flatly that the warriors had not returned with the tribute and the people's promise of loyalty, as expected. I waited for my father to say that wasn't true, but he was silent.

Here a page from the ritual calendar shows one of the sacred 13-day periods. Priests use the sacred calendar to decide when to perform rituals, predict future events, and advise which days would be good for taking on a venture. Each day is known by a number from 1 to 13 combined with a name. The days begin at the bottom left (count the dots), with 1 Flint Knife, and continue along the bottom and up the inner column, ending with 13 Dog.

The gods who rule these 13 days are shown in the middle: on the left is Tonatiuh, the sun god; on the right is Mictlantecuhtli, god of the land of the dead. Between them a man climbs a pole, part of the rituals of the month of *Xocotl huetzi*.

Tlaxochimaco (Offering of Flowers): People gather wildflowers to offer to Huitzilopochtli, the war god. More dancing.

Xocotl huetzi (The Fruit Falls): Feast for the god of fire. Prisoners are sacrificed.

Ochpaniztli (Sweeping): Feast of the earth goddess. Women fight mock battles. Warriors parade before the emperor, who hands out special warrior costumes and weapons.

Panquetzaliztli (The Raising of the Banners): Great feast for Huitzilopochtli. Races, mock battles.

Atemoztli (Water Comes Down): Gods of rain. Young warriors and priests are allowed to fight, as well as raid and loot one another's lodgings.

Tititl (Stretching): A girl clothed all in white is sacrificed to one of the oldest goddesses. Boys are allowed to attack women with sacks.

The Five Useless Days: Time to fast (go without food) and avoid trouble. Evil forces are untamed by rituals, and the world is in danger of ending.

THE EMPEROR'S EDICT

Motecuhzoma the Elder's laws for attire and ornament are still in force. They make clear who everyone is, what each person has accomplished (or not), and who deserves respect (and how much).

While most men wear a cloak knotted at the right shoulder over a loincloth, and most women wear a tunic and long skirt, there are important distinctions to be observed! Penalties are severe.

• Commoners shall not wear cotton; they must make clothes from the fibers of the maguey plant. They must not wear a decorated cloak or one that reaches past their knees (unless they have earned the right with battle scars), or wear sandals in public streets. When in doubt, follow this basic principle: the lowlier you are, the plainer and fewer your clothes. ▶

Maguey Plant

At first I thought I must have misheard the next part. I can barely bring myself to say it now. The men—my father—failed. The war commander took away the symbols of my father's rank: his black-and-yellow cloak with the eyes embroidered along its red border; his helmet with its green feathers—all the clothing that shows who he is.

My father was stone-faced about it, as he is about everything. But when the commander asked if he had anything to say, my father told them strange things, stories he had heard on his travels of hairy-faced strangers and fortresses or mountains that float on the sea. The war commander and his men just looked at each other. I don't think they believed him. My face burned then. All the while my mother stared at the ground and said nothing.

The men left after that. The way they turned their backs on my father, after they'd stripped him of everything that shows who he is—or was—made it clearer than any words that they were leaving him behind, to sit at home like an outcast from their world.

An hour ago I stepped outside to gather the seed jar I'd dropped there earlier, and two of our neighbors looked at me, then quickly glanced away. I know that everyone will look differently at my father now, and at me too.

I keep wondering about those strange tales of his; I wish so much that he hadn't told them. I don't know if those men think my father was making excuses or if they think he's crazy. I know he doesn't lie. But the thought of his words still makes my face burn.

2nd day of Tozoztontli (small vigil), year 1 Reed
Change of Fate

I thought I'd heard the worst, but I was wrong. I found out this morning they're sending me away. It shouldn't be happening yet, and I'm not even going where I always thought I would. My parents used to hint that when I was older I might go to the calmecac, the school that teaches boys to be officials and priests. I knew it must be a reward for my father's bravery. And, they said, I was clever enough to do well there. But that's not where I'm going.

My father told me I'm leaving right away for the House of Youth, where they train warriors. My heart turned heavy as stone.

"There's no better goal for a boy," he said. "It is the surest road

Clothing 2 of 2

• Warriors who have captured a prisoner in battle may wear a decorated cloak. Those who have shown bravery may wear bone necklaces or eagle feathers.

• Priests wear black or dark green cloaks, which may be embroidered with skulls and human bones.

• Only the emperor himself may wear a turquoise cloak.

• A failed warrior may not wear clothes with any color or embroidery, or any jewelry or ornament. A boy at the House of Youth who fails to ever capture a prisoner shall have his head shaved in the tonsure of a "carrier" (an unskilled laborer), the lowliest job.

• Only nobles may wear the most brilliantly colored feathers, gold headbands, greenstones, and other precious gems. Commoners may decorate themselves with rabbit skins or make earrings out of obsidian.

• Well-brought-up girls and women do not paint their faces and may only enhance their looks by keeping clean. For everyday wear (not during festivals), their clothes should be simple, white, and loose, although a little embroidery is allowed.

Attire and Ornament

to success in life and your duty as a Mexicatl." I felt as if he'd put a huge weight on my shoulders. He didn't say I was going because of what had happened to him, and I couldn't ask because I didn't dare speak of it. But I think that must be why.

My thoughts must have shown on my face because he gave me a long look. "Remember," he added, "you do not even belong to us. Your real home is not here. You belong to the gods. Especially to Tezcatlipoca—god of the night sky, of youths, and of war.

"You will go there as I did." And that was the end of it.

My mother of course was silent. That's her way. She often hides what she thinks. She isn't Mexica; she's a Maya, from far away. My father brought her home with him from a campaign long ago. She is very watchful about what she says and does, as if she's stepping around shards of broken pottery.

Tepin put her hand on mine. She's always been able to tell what I'm thinking. I was glad she was there, but I didn't feel like taking her hand, and she let mine drop.

When my mother finally spoke, it was about something completely different. She talked about the days after I was born. They thanked the gods for me, and the midwife said out loud that I had come into the world to fight. They went to a field of battle and buried the cord that had tied me to my mother in the womb. Along with it they buried small arrows and a shield. It's that way with all boy children.

Usually I like those stories, but not this time. Why tell me this again now?

I feel they expect something great of me. To make right what went wrong for my father. As if I could become a great warrior and all would be well.

I keep thinking of the old saying "A Mexicatl is never alone." That's what they've always told me—my father, mother, everyone. It used to make me feel better whenever I was scared or hurt: the idea that not one of us is ever alone, that we are all connected to one another and all belong to the gods. Not just here in Tenochtitlan but all across our empire.

Only, I don't feel that way now. I feel, I don't know—not afraid, but unsure. And there's no one I can talk to about it. I can't talk about that kind of weakness with my mother; in some ways she's like a stranger in our land. My father would never understand; he breathes

THE STORY ALL YOUNG MEXICA LEARN

Our chronicles tell how, long ago, our ancestors left a wonderful place called Aztlan when our god Huitzilopochtli commanded it. The Mexica traveled south through the wild lands, living as hunters and warriors. When they came to this lush valley, all the good land had been taken. Only mosquito-filled swamps were left. But their blazing sun god Huitzilopochtli had made them a promise: when they saw an eagle perched on a cactus, they should stop and build their capital. From there, they would rule and overthrow all others.

The wanderers saw <u>the promised sign of the eagle</u>. But it was on the soggy mudflats of the lake. How could they build an empire on a swampy lagoon? Bit by bit, they filled the marsh with earth and dug canals, trading bulrushes and water creatures for timber and stones from the land-dwelling peoples. They created islands, *chinampas*, on which they tended gardens to grow food.

Now, it's possible the neighbors of these newcomers to the valley remember a different story. They recall barbaric nomads from the north. The violent, savage ways of the Mexica filled them with horror. (Even so, everyone hired the Mexica to fight their battles because their men were so fierce.) For their bad deeds they were chased away onto worse and worse lands around Lake Texcoco, even into an area covered with poisonous snakes, which the Mexica simply roasted and ate. At last they were driven into the lake itself and onto an island. They learned to be self-sufficient because everyone hated them. ▶

The Promised Sign of the Eagle

tenochtitlan

Tenochtitlan 2 of 2

All accounts agree that the Mexica built two cities, Tlatelolco and Tenochtitlan. From their new center of power, they married to make alliances and negotiated more territory. A triple alliance was formed among the Mexica, Texcocans, and Tlacopans. Together they defeated the last competing powers in the valley, and from there undertook wars of conquest to dominate more people and land.

war like air. Tepin, she might have understood once, when she lived here and we were close, but she seems different now—older, and she talks more like a priestess. Anyway, she's leaving tomorrow to return to her temple school. I envy her.

7th day of Tozoztontli (small vigil), year 1 Reed
School of War

I won't fall behind again, I won't fall behind again.

I kept saying those words in my head today, while my heart pounded and my legs ached. While I blinked the sweat away from my eyes. Whatever happens, I won't fail again like I did yesterday.

We fetch and carry water and firewood nearly all day. What this has to do with being a warrior I don't know.

Tochtli, one of the other new boys here, always says, "This is nothing compared to the calmecac." He's small for his age, and sometimes I wonder how he'll keep up, but he doesn't seem worried. He never stops talking. The others groan when he says it, because they've all heard the calmecac stories. So have I, only given the choice I'd be there, so whenever he brings it up I wince inside. Everyone chimes in with some awful detail they've heard—we carry wood and sweep the school, but they have it much worse. They go without food, and the priests punish them by piercing them with thorns. They don't even let the boys sleep through the night! If he had to choose between the House of Youth or calmecac, Tochtli says, he'd take our drudgery any day. They study hard too, he said once, making a face. I wouldn't mind that part. Here, my body's tired all the time, but my mind has nothing to do. In fact, thinking gets me into trouble.

Yesterday we tramped with wood strapped to our backs, our trainer barking at us the whole way. Cipactli is his name; he's a head taller than the other trainers, with shaved temples and a scar running down his cheek that I try not to stare at. He's still a young man, but old enough to have fought in battles. While we struggled forward and he shouted, I let my thoughts wander. Where did he get that scar? I thought of my father's battle stories, and that reminded me of his bizarre tales about strangers and I stumbled. My load of wood lurched to the side, and sticks slid off onto the ground. The boy at my back nearly ran into me. "Move ahead!" Cipactli called. I was scrambling to

TRAINING THE NEXT GENERATION

There are two kinds of schools for Mexica boys—the *calmecac*, run by priests, or the *telpochcalli*, the "House of Youth," run by experienced warriors. Most commoners send their boys to the House of Youth. Some boys start there at age 9, others as late as 15. The calmecac is traditionally only for noble and important families, but sometimes the children of traders and commoners go there too.

CALMECAC FACTS

GOAL: Turn boys into priests or the state's highest officials.
PATRON GOD: Quetzalcoatl, the god of priests, self-sacrifice, and books.
DISCIPLINE: Severe.
PURPOSE OF DISCIPLINE: Achieve self-control and forget about yourself while you serve the Mexica state and its gods.
DAYS: Spent studying, fasting, working hard on the temple land, and helping the priests in their duties. Expect severe punishment for tiny mistakes and learn to cut yourself with thorns to offer your blood to the gods.
NIGHTS: No such thing as a full night's sleep. Get used to being wakened to leave for the mountains to make offerings to the gods.
WHAT YOU LEARN: How to persuade and be a good public speaker. How to count the years and reckon time. Manners such as bows and greetings, holy songs, astrology, interpreting dreams. ▶

HOUSE OF YOUTH FACTS

GOAL: Turn boys into warriors.
PATRON GOD: Tezcatlipoca, "the warrior." Long ago, he used sorcery to drive Quetzalcoatl away from the marvelous city of Tula. Quetzalcoatl has been mad at him ever since, and vowed to come back.
DISCIPLINE: Less harsh than the calmecac.
DAYS: Lots of physical exercise. You may keep company only with warriors, so you'll learn to admire them and love the group life.
NIGHTS: Sleep soundly for the next day's effort, or sing and dance at the House of Song.
WHAT YOU LEARN: How to fight, fit in, and serve the Mexica state.

House of Youth or Calmecac   2 of 2

It's no surprise that the boys from the two schools don't get along. Calmecac students think the telpochcalli boys are rowdy and ignorant, lack respect, and are full of themselves. Telpochcalli members are likely to think the calmecac boys are dull bookworms, sunk in their own gloomy thoughts. They get a chance to fight it out during the month of Atemoztli, when they have mock battles.

As for girls, most commoners attend the local House of Youth for girls, or else their parents may dedicate them to a temple, where they can live for a few years until they are ready to marry and raise children, or stay on and become priestesses. The very old and wise priestesses teach them the art of embroidery and rituals such as offering incense to the gods. The goal of a girl's schooling? To become modest and well behaved, serve the gods, and love and admire her future husband.

pick up the fallen sticks while everyone shot past me. Leaning over made even more wood fall off. What a disaster! Another boy knocked me roughly as he rushed past.

Someone stopped next to me. I looked up to see Matlal. He's a strong boy who doesn't say too much, the kind the trainers like. He grinned and gathered the few remaining pieces in his big hands and shoved them into the pile on my back. Our trainer's shadow fell across us. I glanced at his frowning face and quickly jumped up.

He wasn't watching me, though. "You weren't told to stop," he scolded Matlal. "You must learn to obey before you can lead."

I cringe when I get in trouble. Matlal just nodded seriously, and when the trainer turned he shrugged and grinned again, as if he didn't care. We trotted back to the school side by side.

Stomping alongside the pack of us, Cipactli never stopped shouting: "How will you carry shields, weapons, and food over long distances to fields of battle if you can't carry water and firewood?"

"It's like we never left home," Matlal said, jutting his chin toward our trainer. "He sounds like my father." I forced a smile, out of breath as I was.

We unloaded the wood and I tried to joke with Matlal and the others, but to be honest all I could think of was collapsing somewhere by myself.

It's late now, and quiet. Every boy is lying on his mat, too tired to say much. I'm glad to have made friends with Matlal. Still, he makes me a bit nervous. He's a lot bolder than I am, and in so many ways he's the complete opposite of me. I don't have any reason to think he's mean, but I have a feeling he's the type who senses weakness. Tepin always told me I had good instincts and that I should listen to them. I'll keep my friend, but I'll keep my guard up too.

18th day of Tozoztontli (small vigil), year 1 Reed

Boys and Warriors

So much of the time here I feel like I'm playing a part, pretending to be someone else, and hoping no one will notice.

Yesterday we learned to bind a wound, and today we finally got to handle something other than brooms—Cipactli handed out clubs without blades for practice. The others seem more used to handling weapons than I am, as if they've been playing with them forever. At home I liked the bow and arrow my father gave me, but that was it. I was so clumsy with the club! Worse, I got paired with Matlal for an opponent, and he completely overpowered me. In fact, I think he was a little more heavy-handed than he needed to be. We were just learning how to swing and counter a blow, not trying to batter each other! Afterward he treated it like a joke, and I shrugged and pretended not to notice that he'd been so rough.

I was still panting from practice when Matlal nudged me and pointed past my shoulder. I turned and saw three young men walking toward our trainer. Their warriors' costumes were patterned with jaguar spots, and I knew right away who they were. Those were no ordinary warriors! They'd earned their way into the highest ranks, just like the Eagle warriors. I tried not to stare, but I couldn't help it. Everyone hushed around me; I guess they were staring too. I started to imagine what those men had done to earn their garments. How many battles had they fought? How many prisoners had they captured? Or did it take something more special than that?

THE MEXICA MILITARY ELITE: A GUIDE FOR BOYS IN TRAINING RISING THROUGH THE RANKS

After your first exploit in battle, your long lock of hair will be cut and you'll be called an *iyac*. Now you may grow the rest of your hair long over your right ear.

Once you've captured a prisoner single-handed, you'll be given a cloak decorated with flowers and a plain shield. After two prisoners you may wear sandals to battle, a cone-shaped helmet, and a feathered warrior costume. Four prisoners and you are a *tequiua*. You'll recognize a tequiua by his feather headdress and leather bracelet. He can be a commander and take part in war councils. ▶

I've never thought much about my plain cloak or loincloth. All the boys I knew at home wore the same thing. But suddenly I felt small and bare in my simple clothes. They show everyone what I haven't done; they make it obvious before I speak or try anything.

The Jaguar warriors halted before Cipactli, and from the way they greeted him they obviously knew him well. I heard only bits and pieces of their words, but they were leaving with a large force to crush a rebellion somewhere beyond the valley.

"What makes them forget their place?" I heard Cipactli say, shaking his head in disbelief.

They lowered their voices then, and I didn't catch any more. But Cipactli's usually stoic face lit up in amazement, then settled into a frown. He glanced at all of us staring and raised his hand before one of the Jaguars, cutting his words short. "I mustn't delay you any longer, my friend," he said. The warriors nodded and left him after a quick farewell.

Even Matlal seemed a bit awed. "There's no doubt they're favored by the gods," he muttered. I pictured my father and the scars on his bronze arms. Had he fought alongside men like those? Before his— I don't even know what to call it—his change in fortune. Before, when he was honored too. My face started to burn thinking about it.

Matlal punched my arm. "They started out just like us," he said, then laughed. It seems impossible. The distance between a warrior like

No Ordinary Warriors 2 of 2

To rise in rank it's important to capture formidable opponents—not just barbarians such as the Huaxtecs, but trained warriors from kingdoms such as Tlaxcalla. A warrior's progress reaches its peak at the two highest orders: the Jaguars, known as Tezcatlipoca's warriors, battle in a war costume covered in jaguar spots, their faces visible inside the animal's mouth; and the Eagles, warriors of the sun, don an eagle's-head helmet and feathered warrior costume.

will and victory (that is, the Mexica are winning), the two sides hammer out the terms of surrender: how much tribute will be given, how many men will be offered for sacrifice. The Mexica do not aim to destroy a city or change its way of life or its gods. Tribute is enough to show loyalty to our empire. (Of course, an important portion of tribute will be the feathers and everything else we need to dress our warriors!)

READY FOR BATTLE

To fight, you'll wear close-fitting clothes stuffed with cotton that cover and protect your torso. Helmets, made of paper or feathers, are just for show.

Warriors can find their chief in a battle by looking for his emblem, usually a feathered banner that's held or worn on the back.

Most soldiers carry a round shield made of wood or reeds. They wield a wood sword or club set with sharp pieces of obsidian or flint. They might use a javelin, obsidian-tipped arrows, or very effective slingshots.

GOALS OF WAR

A good warrior always aims to bring his opponent down and avoids dealing a fatal wound. You want to take prisoners who can be sacrificed to the gods! Once the battle clearly shows Huitzilopochtli's

The Two Highest Orders

A WHO'S WHO OF MEXICA DEITIES

We Mexica believe in many gods, and honor them with so many rituals and feast days that it can be hard to believe we have time for anything else! Our gods are not faraway beings in the heavens; they are forces active in everything that lives on earth. Here are some of the most important:

Huitzilopochtli: His name means "Hummingbird of the left, or south." This is the Mexica's patron god, the god of war and of the sun. He demands frequent human sacrifice.

Tezcatlipoca, the "smoking mirror": He sees everything that happens in the world in his obsidian mirror and carries arrows to punish those who commit evil. He takes on more than one form, is everywhere, is all-powerful, and controls human destiny.

Telpochtli: The "young man" is one of the forms taken by Tezcatlipoca, the one in which he protects young warriors. ▶

that and a boy like me is as vast as the sky. But who knows, maybe for some of the others here it's true. No one knows his own destiny, they say. It's all decided the day we're born. Nothing can change it.

1st day of Uey tozoztli (great vigil), year 1 Reed
A Taste of Freedom!

I just heard that tomorrow we'll be set free—for a night. It sounds too good to be true. The Great Vigil begins today. The temples are already filling up with people offering flowers and food to the gods who bring the maize that keeps us alive.

I wonder sometimes about these <u>gods</u> who crave praise all the time and need so many sacrifices to be satisfied. But at least Chicomecoatl is a happy goddess, and her celebrations are cheerful, compared to the rituals for the gods of rain or fire. Why are the gods so ready to crush us the moment we fail? Now, I know these are fool-ish thoughts, and sometimes I worry it's ideas like these that make me different from boys who are born warriors. Better to push them away. At least I know not to share them with the others here.

Anyway, thanks to the gods' feast we'll have some <u>fun and free time</u>, and I'm glad for that. After sunset tomorrow, we'll go to the House of Song. I'm no singer or dancer, but better that than hauling firewood!

2nd day of Uey tozoztli (great vigil), year 1 Reed
Bitter Encounter

I don't know whether I can wait until tonight to get away from here. Or maybe it won't make any difference where I am—I can't disappear, although right now I wish I could.

A group of us were outside the school this morning, cleaning the streets (everyone is anxious to look spotless and ready for the vigil). We were talking and laughing louder than usual, out of earshot of the trainers, and I was feeling happy about our night away from work and sweat.

That didn't last long. Coming from the opposite direction, I saw a winding line of girls headed toward us down the street. Each one held an ear of corn. I knew they must be on their way to the temple of the

Gods 2 of 2

Quetzalcoatl

<u>Quetzalcoatl</u>, the "Quetzal-feathered serpent": The patron of priests, he is the god of learning and knowledge, god of the wind, the evening star (evil), and the morning star (good). He is at odds with Tezcatlipoca.

Tlaloc: God of rain and fertile land. It's very important to honor all the gods who make the earth fertile, so rain will fall and crops will grow.

Centeotl: God of maize. His cult involves the worship of a whole group of gods of sunny warmth, flowers, and feasting. Xilonen is the goddess of the young corn.

Teteoinnan: "Our revered mother." She is the mother of the gods, goddess of earth and of fertility, the patroness of midwives and healers.

Huitzilopochtli (top left), Tezcatlipoca (top right), Tlaloc (bottom right)

Fun and Free Time 1 of 2

POPULAR GAMES AND SPORTS

Looking for ways to play? Mexica love hunting and gambling. Young people especially love dancing. Two of the most popular games are played for fun and betting, but like everything in Mexica life they are linked to the gods and full of sacred meaning: ▶

Fun and Free Time 2 of 2

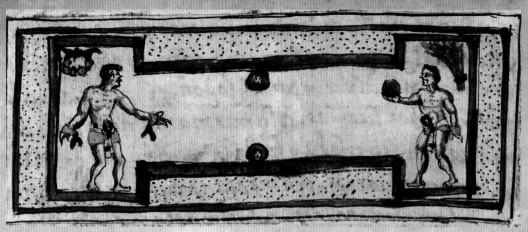

Tlachtli: Only the ruling class may play this ball game. On a long court, two teams face each other on opposite sides of a central line and pass a heavy rubber ball back and forth. Players must hit the ball with their knees or hips—sometimes hands or feet are allowed. If a player can get the ball through one of the two stone rings on the side walls, his team wins. Even though players wear padding for protection, this rough game causes lots of injuries. A statue of Xochipilli ("prince of flowers"), the god of youth, music, and games, sometimes adorns the court. The whole game mirrors the cosmos of the gods: the sky is a great tlachtli court in which gods play with the stars.

Patolli: Anyone can play this one. Four players sit on the ground around a cross-shaped table and throw marked beans onto the board, then move colored stones along the squares. The player who returns to his starting square first wins. The 52 squares represent the 52 years of the sacred and solar calendars combined.

maize goddess. As they got closer, I saw their faces were painted, and their arms and legs were lined with bright feathers, just like the goddess herself. They were free too, instead of staying at home or in the temple school. I looked for Tepin, and smiled when I thought I had spotted her. But it wasn't her.

I was sorry to see that the girl noticed my stare and smile. She tossed her head and whispered to the girl next to her. Her friend smirked. I looked down and started sweeping and wished I could melt into our group.

This part still shames me. The smirking girl reached out as she passed and tugged on the lock of hair that trails down the back of my neck.

"Look, what long hair!" she shouted, so loud I felt as if the whole city could hear. "Another one who's never been to battle! Or is he a girl like us?" They all shrieked with laughter.

I wish I could say I had a ready answer, but it was Matlal who did it for me. "You think you're so precious," he bellowed in that big voice he has. "How would you like to finish off your paintwork with a roll in the mud?"

They shrieked louder and broke into a run. I could hear them laughing even when they were out of sight.

"Don't sulk." Matlal nudged me with his elbow. "We'll be rid of our girlish locks soon enough!"

KNOWING YOUR PLACE IN MEXICA SOCIETY

Every one of the People of the Sun has a role to play in our glorious empire. You're born into your class and it is hard, but not impossible, to move from one group to another.

The emperor stands above everyone else. He is supported by his ruling class: the highest military commanders, the high-priests, the governing officials. A little less exalted, but still highly respected, are all the other warriors and priests.

But there are other roles to play:

Pochteca—Traders and Merchants

Traders are adventurers who set out in caravans to the mysterious lands as far away as the coast. They bring along rabbit fur, embroidered clothes, or gold jewelry to trade, and return with amber, jade, parrot feathers, wild animal skins, even slaves. Many are as tough as warriors because they have to defend their haul against thieves on the way home.

Trading is a job passed from father to son. Pochteca live in their own districts and usually marry someone in their own group. The traders are getting richer all the time, but the smart ones hide their wealth and wear only the plain clothes of commoners. As long as they don't seem like a threat to the ruling class, they'll be left alone to grow wealthy. After all, they travel to distant lands to get all the fine things that adorn the nobles.

▶

I have no wish to fight, but now I'm wondering how long it will be before we're sent to the battlefield. I know I've just begun and it's too early to tell anything. But I also know the longer my hair stays uncut, the greater the shame. And Cipactli has already told us that once a boy goes to battle and has his lock cut, he'll get two, maybe three more chances to impress his commander before he has to give up being a warrior.

So I might fail to become any kind of warrior at all, never mind a Jaguar or an Eagle! I'd be sent home, in disgrace. I'd tend crops or be a common worker. I know that for those who succeed at war, the rewards are huge. My father came from a lowly family, but the day he captured his fourth enemy he became a tequiua, with all sorts of honors and privileges—one of the classes everyone looks up to. And yet, now it looks like he's lost all he gained. Honor or disgrace: is there nothing in between?

3rd day of Uey tozoztli (great vigil), year 1 Reed
Visions in the Dark

What a strange night! I was looking forward to an escape from school, but I got much more than that. I don't even understand the things I saw, so how do I tell about it?

I'll start at the beginning, at the House of Song.

My humiliation yesterday was still on my mind the whole time we were there, watching the dancers whirl in the torchlight. Once the celebrations were over, Matlal and I were walking with the others back to the House of Youth. Tochtli, who always likes to show what he knows, started talking about the calmecac boys who keep a vigil on the mountainside to honor the gods. I was secretly glad we didn't have to do that. Everyone knows nighttime is dangerous. Once the sun god has traveled across the sky and sunk into the land of the dead, all sorts of things are let loose in the world. The old men in my neighborhood used to tell stories of headless creatures and other apparitions people have met in the dark.

I shivered, then said something about the cold air in case they thought I was afraid. When Matlal spoke, my heart sank. "If they can do it, so can we," he said. "Let's cross over the lake and spend the night on the mountainside!" Tochtli mumbled something about night

The Classes 2 of 2

Tolteca—Luxury Artisans

They're less important than the traders, but some have a special mystique: the goldsmiths, for instance, whose art is so adored. Their name comes from a people who lived before the Mexica and left behind much-admired ruins. It's believed their skills have been handed down in a kind of magical kinship. There are many types of artisans, from delicate feather-workers to gem-cutters, who are said to have got their art straight from Quetzalcoatl.

Maceualtin—Commoners

This is by far the biggest class: peasants, laborers, and anyone who doesn't belong to a special class (but who isn't a slave). Commoners who live in the cities are the best off: they pay taxes but get a share of the tribute and have rights. The peasants of the countryside and towns dominated by the Mexica have a slightly harder time. A commoner can always hope to rise in life by becoming a warrior or sometimes a priest. He might get a good job with a noble as a guard or messenger.

Tlatlacotin—Slaves

This is the lowliest group. Male slaves work as unpaid servants or farmhands; women slaves make clothes and cook. But slavery doesn't have to be forever: slaves' children are born free and no law keeps a slave from marrying a free person. People become slaves when they can't pay their debts, or as a punishment for a crime. They may have been captured in battle or offered by their city to the Mexica as part of its tribute; these slaves are likely to be sacrificed.

No matter which class a woman or girl belongs to, her job is to support the men in her family. Some women are respected or feared, though—the priestesses and midwives.

air sapping your strength and shook his head. The other boys with us laughed it off nervously.

I said Cipactli was expecting us back—he did warn us that he'd wake us earlier than ever for training in the morning. Matlal eyed me, and I felt like he was looking through me. "What are you afraid of?" he asked. I thought of the girls' taunts, and of Cipactli's favorite refrain—"Brace your mind and body, strong as an obsidian blade." I don't feel anything like hard stone, but I couldn't let anyone see that. Maybe, I thought, this is the secret. Force yourself.

So I agreed. Matlal grinned and slapped me on the shoulder. "We'll show them," he laughed, tilting his head toward the other boys, who were already moving fast back to the school.

The streets were emptying of revelers. We passed the last stragglers at the water's edge and started onto the deserted causeway, which stretches like a road on stilts over the lake and ends in the darkness on the other side. Even if I haven't been to battle, I reminded myself, at least I can throw myself at a challenge when it's offered me. I'd soon be wishing I hadn't.

The moon had risen by the time we reached the foothills on the other side. I looked back at the shimmering lake, and beyond that the torches moving like fireflies through the city streets. It was a bit comforting. But I felt strange looking at the only home I've ever known from this wilderness—I'd never crossed to this side before. We were past the farmers' marshy plots of land and well into the scrubby brushwood that clings to the foothills like outstretched fingers. We climbed and I wondered what plan Matlal had in mind. None, I suspected, but didn't say so. He was singing. Did he really mean to spend the night out here? I looked around me in the darkness and hoped not. He doesn't think far ahead, I told myself. He'll probably change his mind and we'll go home.

"Look," Matlal hissed suddenly, and I jumped.

My eyes followed his pointing hand. Away from the city, across the lake, was the dim shape of hills. At first I saw nothing and guessed he was teasing. Then I just barely caught a brief flicker of light.

"There!" he said. "Did you see?" I nodded, my throat too tight and dry to speak.

RESISTING MEXICA POWER

Tlaxcalla, that stubbornly independent territory east of Tenochtitlan on the other side of the mountains, is one of the few holdouts against the mighty Mexica empire. The Mexica have surrounded this kingdom and cut off its trade with the outside world, but have never defeated it. Tlaxcallans are the Mexica's archrivals and they command respect. Tlaxcalla's warriors are an especially great prize to capture and sacrifice. On grand occasions of celebration, the Mexica emperor likes to invite Tlaxcallan nobles, because what's the point of flaunting your power if your enemy is not there to see it?

Tlaxcalla's warriors

The light glowed again, and for an instant I made out a moving shape, something like a giant snake in the hills. A shiver, not from the cold, ran through me. I was thinking of those old stories of night apparitions.

"What kind of monster is that?" I blurted out before I could stop myself.

Matlal shook his head. "That's no monster—it looks like a line of people, moving through the hills. When they reach a peak, we can see their torches."

I felt foolish. I was glad that at least Matlal hadn't laughed. He seemed too fascinated by the sight. "What are they doing?" I asked quickly. "There's nothing but small villages out there. And beyond that, just hills between us and the kingdom of Tlaxcalla. Could they have come from there?"

What did it mean? We looked at each other, but neither of us had an answer.

"Let's go back to the school," I said, feeling breathless. "We should tell Cipactli." To my relief, Matlal agreed right away.

Cipactli was still awake when we returned, and ready to scold us for being late. We told him our story about the moving lights. I know we sounded excited and kept interrupting each other. I wondered if Cipactli would laugh at us or accuse us of falling asleep and dreaming. But his face got very stern and serious, and his eyes narrowed. It made me feel alarmed.

WHY DO WE FIGHT IT?

You boys in training may wonder about these contests we undertake against those "not of our house."

The Flower Wars, or *xochiyaoyotl*, are battles arranged between the Mexica and other peoples, mostly the Tlaxcallans. This never-ending contest is a way to train young warriors, keep experienced ones sharp and ready for real war, and give impatient youths the chance to earn glory. Most important, they are a means of capturing prisoners who can be sacrificed to our gods.

Long ago, a terrible famine nearly destroyed the Mexica, and the priests agreed it was because sacrifices to the gods had been too few. The leaders of our triple alliance (the Mexica, Texcoco, and Tlacopan) decided that whenever there was no war going on, we would fight anyway, against the warriors of Tlaxcalla, Huexotzinco, and Cholula. There must never again be a shortage of victims for the temples because the consequences would be terrible: the sun would stop in its path across the sky, the earth would stop giving food, the world itself would come to an end.

When our emperor was asked why we don't just conquer Tlaxcalla, he said, "We could easily do so; but then there would be nowhere left for the young men to train, except far away; and, also, we ▶

I was curious enough to be bold and asked Cipactli what he thought it meant.

He gave a start and looked at me a moment before answering. "Nothing that is for you to know, not now," he said. "Say nothing to the others." But I noticed he forgot all about our lateness and any punishment he had in mind for us.

He sent us to our mats to sleep, but I know I'll be awake for a long time. I don't believe it means nothing, and I can tell Matlal doesn't either.

9th day of Tlaxochimaco (offering of flowers), year 1 Reed
First Combat

I wish I could live this day over and undo what should never have happened. But that's impossible.

When I first heard, I didn't believe it. We were really going. Leaving with the men for a battle. Cipactli gathered us together and told us that some of us would be chosen to go with the warriors to the Flower War. I'd known that war captains and trainers took boys into the field with them so they could learn, but I didn't expect it so soon! The fighting would be against the warriors of Tlaxcalla. Matlal and I shot glances at each other. Did this sudden war game have anything to do with what we'd seen?

I thought right away—I won't be chosen; I was so useless in weapons training. The idea made me feel relieved and, at the same time, a bit disappointed. Boys were cheering when their names were called—including Matlal, but that was no surprise to anyone. When Cipactli called my name next, my mouth fell open. I stayed speechless while Matlal and the others whooped and shouted all around me.

Cipactli spoke with respect of the Tlaxcallan warriors we were about to face. He called them hardy and fearless, true prizes to capture. That night he told us the story of one of their greatest warriors, Tlahuicole. I'd heard his name before. He was captured by the Mexica, but his reputation was so great they made him an offer: they wouldn't sacrifice him if he'd lead the Mexica army in battle. He took the command and won the victory for the Mexica. But as soon as he returned, he insisted on being taken to the temple and sacrificed. He knew his fate had only been delayed, not changed, Cipactli said, and he met it without flinching.

Capturing Prisoners

Flower War 2 of 2

wanted there always to be people to sacrifice to our gods."

The clever among you may realize there is another benefit to fighting Flower Wars. Constant fighting keeps opponents weak. Who could continually fight us, with our huge population and army, without sapping their own strength? Who knows—given time they may also be forced into submission and become part of the empire.

Land ruled by the Mexica and their allies

We left at dawn. Cipactli was dressed for war, wearing his helmet and thick cotton-stuffed tunic to ward off the blows of weapons. My head was still reeling from being chosen, but I was even more astonished when Cipactli turned to me and gave me his round wooden shield to carry. I saw the scars of blows on it.

"Stay close to me," he said. "We'll see if you are your father's son."

We tramped along the roads out of the city, maybe 20 of us young ones mixed among the older boys, the masters of youth, and the hundreds of warriors in their feathered war costumes. In the crowd I spotted the shaved heads of Otomí warriors, who fight in pairs and vow never to step backward in battle, and many rope-bearers, who stay at the ready to tie up prisoners. Traders in their canoes stared as we crossed the causeway over Lake Texcoco.

It was late morning when we reached the field of contest, a sun-parched stretch of grassy plain. The Tlaxcallan army was waiting at a distance, like opponents on a tlachtli court. Only I knew this was not a ball game—it was much more serious, and dangerous. I won't hide that I was glad to be sent to the sidelines. It looked like we would just watch and wait for a command to help with something small. Matlal sulked. He'd been given ropes to carry. "We didn't come here to stand still and do nothing," he complained, but I didn't share his disappointment.

When the fighting began, it was fierce and so close that my ears were filled with the shouts of men and the pounding of my own blood. Right in front of me—I could have reached out and touched them—two warriors brought down a Tlaxcallan with ruthless blows to his legs. His scream pierced my ears. I knew then how real this fight was—we'd left the world of practice behind. After that, there was so much confusion I couldn't spot Cipactli anymore among all the struggling warriors.

I remember the faces of the other boys, all set in fierce frowns, but I felt only panic. You're still young, I told myself. There's no shame in not fighting. Not yet.

All at once the wailing noise of conches and shrieks from bone whistles filled the air. For a few seconds dust stirred up by running feet screened everything from my sight. Then I heard a boy shouting, "We have put them to flight! They're on the run!"

That's when it happened. I've tried to slow it down in my mind to remember the details—it was all so fast. I remember choking on the dust. It stung my eyes, and I squeezed them shut. When I opened them again I searched for Matlal in the clouds of sand. Bodies shoved me as they passed. I was blind, confused—useless!

The dust cleared a little and I saw a group of fleeing men in unfamiliar clothes. Tlaxcallans! The next instant I nearly collided with a breathless Tlaxcallan youth. He was thin-faced and lanky and, I noticed, his long arms held no weapon. I froze, and for a moment we stared at each other. His black, deep-set eyes looked as surprised as I felt.

The thunder of stomping feet and the clatter of shields all at once grew louder. I sensed we were about to be trampled by another wave of running men. I dove out of the way, grabbing the boy's arm to pull him along. We hit the sand side by side, just out of the path of pounding feet.

Maybe the fall knocked sense into my skull. I suddenly thought, I just did everything a warrior must never do. I bolted when I should have stood my ground. I helped my enemy!

The next thing I remember Matlal was back, shouting in my ear. "This is our chance—they've run the wrong way!" When he saw the boy next to me his eyes widened. "You! You got one!" he sputtered.

The young warrior sprang up. I hesitated, but Matlal was on him in a flash, knocking him back down. "Come on!" Matlal ordered me. "Do you want to wear that lock forever?"

I grabbed the boy's wrists, trying to play my part. I began to realize what an incredible chance Matlal was offering me. An escape from my mistake, for sure, but even more than that. Matlal thought my blundering was bravery, that I was trying to take a prisoner. It wasn't true—it was ridiculous, I knew—but I played along.

We tied his wrists and ankles, and then headed for the Mexica camp with our prize between us.

"What's your name?" I asked, because I didn't know what else to say.

The boy jerked his head up and looked straight at me. "Zolin," he said. His dark eyes were moist with tears now, and his face looked younger than it had at first. His stare accused me. I tried to look back, but I couldn't stand it and lowered my eyes almost at once. When I looked up again Matlal was watching me and frowning a little, as if I puzzled him.

The warriors were already streaming back to camp. We led the Tlaxcallan boy to Cipactli, who stood with dust and sweat streaking his body like rivers. I saw a blood-stained cloth on his arm, and only then did I notice the smell that filled the air: the blood of wounded men. It made me light-headed, and I clenched my fists to steady myself.

Cipactli nodded approvingly but cut Matlal's excited story short. He ordered two warriors to take our captive. I watched as they led him away to join a line of grim-looking prisoners. He glanced back at us, and this time I avoided his stare.

I turned to Cipactli instead and asked him what would happen to the prisoners. He looked surprised at my interest. "Most will become slaves," he told me. "But," he added, "a few lucky ones will have a far greater destiny, one the gods chose for them the day they were born."

I knew what he was going to say next, and even in the late-day sun I felt suddenly cold. "They will meet their end on the sacrificial stone of our great temple," he said, "and join the warriors who serve the sun god, the Turquoise Prince, the soaring eagle. There is no greater destiny." Cipactli looked at me and almost smiled. "You have done well today," he said, and walked away.

It's all over now and we're back at the House of Youth. All the way home I had a strange feeling I couldn't get rid of. A feeling that something is terribly wrong. And a fear keeps racing through me. What if Matlal ever suspects the truth about what I did?

15th day of Tlaxochimaco (offering of flowers), year 1 Reed
False Warrior

I've made up my mind. I know what I have to do; I just need the courage to do it. It wasn't obvious to me at first, but it is now. At first all I could think about was that I'm a fraud.

They cut our locks. A slice of the flint knife sent my black hair to the ground. I should have been rejoicing, but I was uneasy inside. Matlal was laughing and rubbing his bare neck. I tried to smile too.

Lots of boys had their locks cut. They shouted and slapped one another on the back. I scanned the faces of those boys who'd stayed behind and still wore their long hair. Tochtli looked envious, others shame-faced, and they watched silently. They envy me, I was thinking, but they shouldn't.

I wanted so much to laugh like the others and enjoy the moment, but in my heart I knew I was an impostor. I felt doubt inside me every time Matlal glanced my way. Did he suspect? We're having a feast tonight, and while everyone was getting ready I saw Matlal talking alone with Cipactli. He knows, I thought, he's telling him. I had to stop myself from bolting.

My childish hair is gone, but I don't feel like a warrior. I panicked in the middle of a battle; I nearly fainted at the sight and smell of blood! Last night I dreamed about our captive boy's eyes. They could have been the eyes of any of the boys here. He was no different, and not much older than I am.

We share the same god now, Zolin and I—Tezcatlipoca, the lord of slaves and of young warriors. Strange! Cipactli told me something else too. Zolin won't be a slave for long. He'll surely be chosen to be sacrificed at our great temple. Part of me wishes he'd been left in slavery. That's a shameful wish, I know. Sacrifice is a great destiny, just as Cipactli says, and so I've often been told. I've seen victims chosen for sacrifice, dressed like the gods they're offered to, making their way to the temple, surrounded by dancers and singers. But I've never known one or faced one up close, looked into his eyes. I can still picture the way he walked between me and Matlal. He was the brave one, not me.

There's one thing that's very clear to me now. I'm no warrior and I never will be. It's what every boy wants, I know, or should want. But I don't believe the flesh and blood I'm made of can be molded into a fighter. I'm not afraid of working hard or of getting hurt. But to wield a spear, to face shouting enemies in battle, to stop being who I am and become one fierce animal along with all the others—I just don't *believe* it can happen. (These are also shameful thoughts, I know. Unworthy of a warrior's son. Which is what I am.)

The more I think about it, the surer I am that Matlal told Cipactli I'm a failure. No, worse, a traitor. It will come sooner or later, the punishment, the shame. What will that do for my father? It will be a hundred times worse for him to have a son accused too.

MAKING SURE THE WORLD GOES ON

A public reminder from the priests of Huitzilopochtli

The world we live in is not the first. There were four worlds before this one, each better than the last. Now our world is in danger of ending at any time. Don't despair: we have it in our power to delay the catastrophe. The answer is to keep sacrificing to the gods.

The gods sacrificed greatly to give the world its sun and to create humans. People are in their debt. First, one of the gods threw himself into a fire and became the sun. To get the new sun started across the sky, the other gods gave their own blood. Now humans must do the same to keep the sun moving— blood is the most valuable gift we can offer because it is the water of life. Likewise, for rain to fall, for the seasons to keep following one another, human blood must be offered to the gods.

Often the victim is dressed as the god who is to be honored. Sometimes they get to live in great wealth like a lord for a year before the ceremony. During some festivals they might dance right up until the fatal moment.

The sacrifice itself usually takes place like this: the victim is led up the steps of the temple with great ceremony and is grabbed by the priests at the final moment. He is stretched out on his ▶

back on a stone, while four priests hold his arms and legs. A fifth priest removes the victim's heart with a flint knife. Sometimes the victim is tied to a large stone on a length of rope and given wood weapons to fight a series of warriors.

Remember, sacrificial victims, like warriors who die in battle or women who die in childbirth, enjoy a special afterlife. For four years they accompany the sun each day on his glorious course. The men lead the way to the sun's zenith; the women bring it to its setting in the evening. When four years have passed, the warriors become carefree hummingbirds or swarms of butterflies, enjoying the sun's warmth and sipping the nectar of flowers in a never-ending feast. The women's fate is less wonderful: they become much-feared spirits who can harm the living.

What of everyone else? Some people are marked by the rain god Tlaloc: those who drown or are struck by lightning go straight to a warm paradise of flowers. For the rest, the afterlife is somber. The dead person's spirit wanders for four years searching for its final home in the cold and dark underworld, Mictlan. It is ruled by the god Mictlantecuhtli and his wife, Mictlancihuatl, who are always surrounded by owls and spiders.

All day I've been haunted by one thought: Zolin is going to be sacrificed *because of me*. And then I realized what the trouble is. The victim is supposed to be a warrior, captured by another warrior. But I didn't capture Zolin at all. I wasn't even trying to. It was a mistake.

What if it isn't his fate to be a sacrifice at all? Then my blunder would send the wrong person to the sacrificial stone. How can the gods be pleased with that? But it's not too late. I can still make right what I've done wrong.

I can set him free. Slaves have escaped before—I just need to help him a little. At first I couldn't figure out how. I have no excuse to see him; I can't imagine why someone like me would be let anywhere near the victims.

I felt hopeless. But then I realized—it seems so obvious now! I can't approach them, but priests or priestesses can. Or their students, like Tepin.

She could help me if she wanted to. After the feast, when everyone is sleeping here, I'll go, just before dawn. I'll sneak away to the temple and see her. I hope she'll understand, the way she used to.

16th day of Tlaxochimaco (offering of flowers), year 1 Reed
Tepin's Omens

It can be hard to see how small things are connected to great ones, but sometimes it becomes clear and you see the whole design at once. Maybe the world is like a web, and one person's actions can have vast consequences. Pluck at one point and the whole thing shakes, or tears apart. I took the first steps in my plan today, and I think I see now how important it is that I not fail in the rest.

When I entered the temple school, I wondered if anyone would challenge me, but no one did. Everyone I passed seemed too busy to notice me. I didn't think too much about what was distracting them all—I wanted to find Tepin. She seemed changed that last time I saw her at home, but when we were younger I could always talk to her.

I wandered a little and found her in an antechamber next to the sanctuary. She was crouched down on her heels, looking at a parchment stretched on the ground. A broom was lying beside her. Luck is with me today, I thought. A good sign.

How to Write in Pictures

AN INTRODUCTION FOR TEMPLE STUDENTS

The scribe, who must be a good painter, has everyone's respect. He works for the temples, the courts of law, or the royal government. His art might seem mysterious to those ignorant of writing, but it works like this:

You paint small pictures of the things you want to show (a person, an ear of maize), as well as pictures that stand for ideas (a burning temple means defeat, or conquest; water and fire mean war). It's important to use the right colors for each word.

Once you know your picture-symbols, you can use them to represent the same sound in another word that has nothing to do with the symbol. So, you write the sound "mi" by drawing an arrow *(mitl)* in a word that has nothing to do with arrows.

The scribe's writing does not exactly follow our language, Nahuatl, as it is spoken. It just sums up important things so they're not forgotten. You'll have to learn all the important songs and stories by heart.

A burning temple is the symbol for "defeat" or "conquest."

The pictures before each burning temple stand for place names. Together they make a list of cities conquered by the Mexica.

Tepin must have heard my footsteps. She turned around and gasped when she saw me, then covered her smile with her hand, like she used to. She stared at my hair. "You're a warrior now," she said.

"Not yet …" I started to say, then shrugged and looked down. How could I explain to her about my plan? I started to doubt whether I even should. Instead I pointed at the parchment on the floor and asked her if she was studying how to write in pictures, like the priests do.

Tepin nodded and looked happy that I'd asked. I scanned the colorful pictures of people, buildings, and animals. I pointed out a picture of a temple in flames and asked her what it meant. That, she told me, was the picture for "defeat."

"This parchment tells the story of the Mexica," she said matter-of-factly, "so it's a story of war." Everywhere I turn, the same thing! How many temples have burned across the world, I wonder, so that the Mexica could rule it?

"Is war the only story?" I blurted out. Tepin looked surprised, and I tried to make light of it. "Maybe you're the one who should have gone to the House of Youth," I said, forcing a laugh. "You're stronger than I am."

Tepin didn't laugh. She shook her head. "I've been afraid too, since I came here. Don't be discouraged, you get over it." That sounded more like the old Tepin.

"But what if I—what if someone—can't?" I asked. "I mean, what if a boy *can't* become a warrior?"

Tepin sighed and tilted her head. "Well, that's not a noble fate. But these things are in the hands of the gods."

Now she sounded like everyone else again. We were quiet for a moment and then, like she used to, Tepin seemed to read my thoughts. "Did you know that our emperor, the great Motecuhzoma himself, didn't believe he would be a warrior? When he was young, he thought he would be a priest. It was his brother who was trained to fight and to rule. When his brother lost his life in battle, his destiny changed. He had no choice either."

I didn't answer, so she went on. "I know—they ask many hard things of us. A wrong step one way or the other and we plunge into darkness and disgrace. Our right path is narrow and difficult and laid out for us. But we carry a great gift as we walk: we know who we are and we are never alone."

Then she said something that startled me, and it's troubled me ever since. "And now," she added, "it's more important than ever to be strong together." I asked her what she meant.

She told me of bizarre things that have been happening—signs in the skies, on the earth. A star that streaked across the sky in the middle of the day; a temple that burst into flames, another struck by lightning. The priests know they are clues about the fate of the empire. Tepin didn't know their meaning, but she said everyone whispers about some crisis that is surely coming.

In my mind I ran through all the odd things I know about—what Matlal and I saw in the mountains, my father's stories of strange beings. Something is definitely wrong.

Tepin grabbed my arm and said, "Let's walk." Maybe she was worried someone was listening, because she whispered as she told me of priests who were put to death when they could not explain the meaning of the star. It worried the emperor terribly. Now he wants everyone's dreams reported to him.

It sounds like everything is being shaken loose from its natural place in the world. I started to wonder—what's causing it? Are the gods angry? And wasn't I just making matters worse with my mistake?

I knew then I had to tell Tepin. I halted in the narrow passage she was leading us through, and she stopped too, looking at me. Before

Lord of the People of the Sun

Motecuhzoma Xocoyotzin has been the Mexica's ruler for 17 years. In the year 10 Rabbit, he inherited a huge empire and somewhere between 11 million and 20 million subjects. The empire he rules is a great military power, yet Motecuhzoma trained to be a priest. It was his brother who had been taught how to lead an army, keep the vast empire under control, and carve out even more territory to dominate. Even so, everyone's first impressions of the new emperor were good: in speech, he seemed determined and moderate, two qualities the Mexica admire.

Our emperor lives in great luxury in his palace in Tenochtitlan. The palace is so big it's like a town in itself, with many entrances for those on foot or in boats. People who visit it say that each time they go, they walk around until they're tired and still have not seen it all. On the ground floor are all the governors, judges, and commanders who run the empire. The emperor's rooms are on the second floor. Musicians are on hand at all times; a house of birds contains all the winged species of the empire to delight the emperor with songs; pumas and jaguars are kept in cages. At night, noble young warriors come from the local schools to sing and dance. It's said that each day more than 300 dishes are prepared for Motecuhzoma, and from this array he chooses which ones he would like. (Leftovers are given to the palace guards.)

For the last 10 years, the emperor, always sensitive to prophesies and dreams, has been troubled by omens. Now stories of fortresses on the sea coming from the east fill him with dread.

TIPS FOR VISITORS, FROM YOUR LOCAL POCHTECHA

Whether you are a rugged Huaxtec with animal hides to sell or a rich trader with a canoe full of jade necklaces, sooner or later you'll find your way to the markets of Tenochtitlan.

The city has many squares with markets, but the biggest (and best) is in Tlatelolco, Tenochtitlan's twin city (once a rival Mexica city, it was finally dominated by the Mexica of Tenochtitlan). The Tlatelolco market is in a huge square near the great temple, surrounded on all sides by covered galleries. Up to 25,000 people come each day to buy and sell, but every five days there is an even greater market with a crowd of up to 50,000. People move slowly and no one shouts, so the constant noise of murmurs is like a steady hum.

Every Mexicatl loves to go to market, just to look around and gossip and be ▶

I could have second thoughts, I told her what had happened at the Flower War, about Zolin, everything. And in a whisper I told her what I want to do and asked for her help. She didn't seem sad for me or ashamed, like I'd feared. She got angry.

How could I think about interfering with Zolin? she demanded, her temper flaring. Didn't I care at all about the gods—or our father? I was stunned. What did he have to do with it?

Voices at the end of the passage made us both jump. Tepin pulled me farther along, away from the torchlight.

"If we got caught," she whispered, "we'd do even more damage to our father's reputation. His fate is uncertain. Some believe him, but others want to blame him. We'd be putting a weapon into the hands of those who attack him if we did anything shameful."

My face got hot. I hadn't thought of that. But my instincts still told me that this mistake of mine had to be made right. I reminded her of the omens and told her about what I'd seen in the mountains.

"If the wrong person is sacrificed, if the one fated for sacrifice is spared, how will that please the gods who are so obviously giving signs that things are wrong in the world? It will insult them!"

Tepin looked skeptical. I could tell she didn't like me telling her what would please the gods or not—she was the one in the temple, not me. Yet I could see her wavering. "It's not a thing our father would want us to do," she said, shaking her head. "Or our mother."

Our mother? That made me think of something. "Maybe she would," I said quietly. Tepin shot a surprised look at me. "Think of her," I went on, "how sad she seems sometimes, far from her people and homeland. Even after all this time. How would someone feel if they were taken away from everything they know, but by mistake?"

She looked down and was quiet, and I kept silent, not wanting to make her angry at me again. It was the right thing to do, because after a moment she nodded slowly.

Tepin had to leave me for a while to take part in the temple's daily rituals. But she promised to meet me later in the marketplace. In the meantime she'll find out where those prisoners handpicked for sacrifice are being held.

Tezcatlipoca, Zolin's god and mine, help me now.

The Marketplace 2 of 2

where everything is happening. <u>Merchants</u> sell the wonderful things they bring home from "beyond the mists," as they call faraway places: turquoise, jade, and shells from the distant ocean, gold and silver jewelry, multicolored feathers (all Mexica adore feathers). Farmers from the chinampas, the gardens around the city, bring their maize, flowers, chilies, and tomatoes by canoe along the canals. Specialists offer more exotic fare: frog and green chilis, gophers with sauce, or you can pick up one of the hairless dogs that make a popular tasty dish. Slaves are brought here for sale too, but it is also their chance to break for freedom. Only their owner or his son may try to stop them.

Official market guardians wander through the crowds, watching how the merchants measure and sell. Everyone buys and sells by barter, trading one thing for another. You can buy what you need with cacao beans, thin copper axes, or gold dust carried in feather quills. Cloaks are good, but bring a lot of them if you want to buy something expensive. A slave is worth 30 to 40 cloaks; you can get a canoe for one cloak.

Although the marketplace is amazingly orderly for its size, it has its dangers. Unwanted Tenochtitlan youths once wandered into the Tlatelolco market at a time when the cities were rivals. They were asked sinisterly, "Have you come to sell your intestines or your hearts?" Best to keep your eyes and ears open and your wits about you as you wander through.

But once you've been here, you're sure to come back. Every Mexicatl does. Old women whose legs can barely carry them have been known to use their last bit of strength to get to the market!

Merchants

17th day of Tlaxochimaco (offering of flowers), year 1 Reed
Broken Cages

It's over. I tell myself that I've done all I can, his fate is out of my hands now.

I waited for Tepin by the bird-sellers in the market, where we used to love to go. It felt like ages were passing and still she didn't come. I started to regret choosing that place; the squawking and flapping was making me even more nervous.

At last I saw her, all in white, heading steadily and quickly for me, as if she didn't want to give herself time to change her mind. She was clutching wreaths of wildflowers, like the ones they drape around the neck and head of the victim of the feast of Tezcatlipoca.

She told me in a low, excited voice that a whole procession of captives was on its way toward us. Now! Flower War prisoners and slaves offered by rich merchants had been bathed and dressed in the early morning. They'd be sure to pass through the marketplace on their way to the temple of Tezcatlipoca.

I was stunned by her words. I'd thought our rescue would be carried out in some secret, hidden place, not out here, in front of a thousand pairs of eyes!

"This is better—" she started to say, probably seeing the panic on my face, but the buzz of voices around us grew louder. Looking up, I saw a boisterous procession pushing its way through the marketplace. Warriors strode alongside girls bearing baskets of flowers, and at the center of the throng walked captives, freshly washed and decorated. People from the market crowded around, excited.

When I saw him among the captives, looking dazed, I felt that twinge of guilt all over again. I had seen this before. For days leading up to the ceremony, and sometimes for much longer, captives parade and dance, flattered and fussed over. They always look exhausted. No ropes bind them, but they're always flanked and guarded by masters of youth from the warrior schools.

"Tepin, it's him," I said, pointing Zolin out to her. "What are we going to do?"

She grabbed my hand and led me toward the line. A warrior pushed me back, but he let Tepin slip under his arm. She joined the throng of girls dancing around the captives, and I watched as she threaded her way through them. She reached up to put a wreath around Zolin's neck, and he bent forward obediently, as if he expected it.

She started dancing with him. I got impatient—what was she doing? At first he ignored her, but then he put his hands in hers and let her lead him in an awkward dance. I could see that with every step she drew him slowly out of the inner throng of slaves. Soon they were dancing alongside the group, blending into the crowd of curious onlookers.

The masters of youth were scanning the crowd. That's not good enough, Tepin, I thought. They'll see him. One of them was staring directly at their backs.

It was agony to watch and wait; I had to do something. I looked around me at the cages of birds and on impulse I grabbed the side of one cage and yanked hard, pulling it over. That sent them all toppling, smashing open. Birds flew out, shrieking. The merchants were shouting. One lunged for me, and I ran.

The commotion spread to the procession, where people covered their heads against the wings and beaks of the escaping parrots. Merchants ran among the priests and captives.

I looked for Zolin and saw him, now standing still, glancing around, startled. Tepin had left his side and was nowhere in sight. Why didn't he run? I couldn't understand it.

His eyes fastened on me. Run, I mouthed. Still he didn't move. *Run*, I mouthed again, but it was like a scream inside me.

Then, as if a stronger voice had commanded it, he suddenly sprang forward, tearing through the crowd, weaving like a deer.

Priests and warriors were rounding up the scattered captives, but the confusion hadn't stopped. Now I spotted Tepin and looked at her triumphantly. She nodded seriously. We parted quickly, and when I slipped back to the House of Youth I got a mild scolding. Everyone was still in the mood to celebrate, so there was no punishment.

It wasn't long before the school was buzzing with stories of what had happened in the marketplace. "A prisoner from the Flower War has escaped," I heard a trainer say. "No," someone else interrupted, "at least 10 are gone!" They argued. I said nothing and tried to look as surprised as the others.

Tochtli was excited. "The law says that if a lucky one can run all the way to the emperor's palace, he will be freed!"

"Lucky—and fast," Matlal laughed.

I hope in my heart Zolin made it. Tezcatlipoca, let it be so.

1st day of Xocotl huetzi (the fruit falls), year 1 Reed
Two Missions

We're leaving again, and this time it's no war game. And that's not the only surprise I had today.

Cipactli told us all that the people of Tlaxcalla, long intimidated by our power, are growing bold. They've been moving in large numbers into the valley around our Lake Texcoco. Maybe that's what Matlal and I saw in the mountains—a Tlaxcallan army on the move!

The recent escape of Tlaxcallan prisoners from our capital, Cipactli added, is like a slap in our face. I froze as he spoke, but he never looked at me. And, he went on to say, they're not the only ones making trouble. Mexica forces are already marching out of the capital to crush a rebellion. We're about to join a major force leaving Tenochtitlan. It's all happening so fast my head is spinning.

Rumors have been flying around. Scouts returned to the city at a run, talking of uprisings at the edges of the empire, near the Great Sea.

No one could explain what had made our subjects so defiant, but the scouts repeated bizarre stories they said were swirling through those lands like a wind that makes people lose their senses. Extraordinary beings were sighted on the shores of the sea. They came in canoes bigger than anything anyone had ever seen. Their skin was very pale, their faces hairy. Some rode long-legged beasts, like <u>deer</u> without antlers.

Deer

Of course, right away I thought of my father's tales. So did some of the other boys. It seems a lot of them know about his reports but haven't said anything to my face before now. Tochtli nudged me. "I guess you know at least one person who believes those stories!" He had a mischievous gleam in his eyes. I was surprised; Tochtli always seemed so friendly. Maybe he's still jealous of my false honors. Some of the others laughed.

At first I wanted to disappear, but when I realized my father made me ashamed, I got angry. Not just at them but at myself for being disloyal.

I told them that if my father said something, you could count on it being true. I repeated something I'd heard people say: the strange apparitions and the rebellions were probably connected. A couple of boys stared wide-eyed and seemed to believe me, but they were younger ones, the kind who are easily frightened.

I've avoided Matlal ever since the Flower War—I can't help it, I keep imagining he knows. But now I hoped he'd take my side, for friendship. It's easy to stand your ground when at least one friend stands by you. But he shrugged and seemed unconvinced either way. He tried to make light of it all. I could see I was alone. How quick people are to switch to the side that seems to be winning the most friends!

I squirmed. "Well," I said, "who knows what the witnesses my father questioned really saw." I wanted to let them know that he wasn't the only one who spoke of these things, but I was also hinting that he never said he believed the stories, he only reported other people's words. Matlal tilted his head to the side and eyed me silently, and I felt more disloyal than ever.

I didn't notice Cipactli arrive during all this, but he suddenly interrupted us in his loud voice, saying rumors were for fools, that a warrior does as he's told and doesn't distract himself with dreams and fantasies.

When I turned to look at Cipactli, I nearly jumped. Behind him stood my father. What was he doing here? Had he heard us talking?

Cipactli beckoned to me, and I was nervous as I went to them. Cipactli put his hand on my shoulder and turned to my father. "I took him young to the Flower War," he said. "Minds and limbs are best shaped when new—that's what you taught me."

Taught him? My father saw my surprised face and smiled. "I trained Cipactli. And he has fought alongside me since then. Now we sometimes seek each other's counsel." Cipactli nodded, looking pleased about the compliment. "He's a fine warrior," my father said to me. "Listen to him."

If he had overheard any of the boys he didn't say. As always, he kept his words to what was most important. For a moment I hoped he was here because he was coming with us, but that wasn't the case. He'd come to see Cipactli, who, he said, had long been "his eyes and ears," to learn what my trainer had heard of the rebellions. But my father was being sent with scouts to our subjects in Zautla, to confirm their loyalty and secure their help. My heart drooped at this. They were sending him far from the center of the conflict. Was that less honorable? It must be, but I couldn't ask him that.

He brushed his hand over my shorn nape and nodded with a satisfied look. "I heard of your bravery. That is a story you'll always remember. You must tell it to me someday." I swallowed and forced myself to meet his gaze. He glanced at the boys behind me. "A warrior need never fear telling any story that is true."

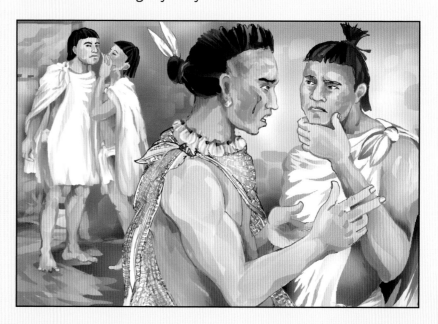

He's gone now. Once he'd left, Cipactli gave us a typical lecture: "Leave as if abandoning all behind. Many depart today; some will not return. All are in the hands of the gods."

Not very comforting words, at least not to me.

3rd day of Xocotl huetzi (the fruit falls), year 1 Reed
A Fateful Choice

A person can have more than one face it seems. I've seen a new one, on a friend I thought I knew. But even that doesn't seem important now, in this awful place where fate has cast me.

We left Tenochtitlan days ago. But we never made it to our destination; we barely got past the mountains. A trap was waiting for us on the way. They sprang on our column as we passed through a narrow gorge. They must have been hiding in the hills, and rushed with the sun behind them to blind us. Totonacs—people long ruled by the Mexica.

They fell on us like heavy rain. Hundreds of warriors, ferocious-looking with their painted faces, crying out all together in a noise to deafen us. We were ordered to retreat before they could wrap around us and cut off our only way out. I didn't think I had learned anything at the Flower War. But this time, strangely, I didn't panic or feel as blind.

Arrows and javelins flew at our backs, and I spotted Cipactli among the last of the retreating warriors, urging us ahead. An instant later I saw him sink to the ground. I turned and ran back to him. A spear had glanced off his thigh and he was bleeding. I tore a piece of cloth from his cloak and started to bind the wound, just as I'd been taught. I'd practiced it so many times I didn't even think about it. Everything fell into place.

I knew we had to catch up with the others. How would I get Cipactli moving? From the corner of my eye, I spotted Matlal scrambling up the hillside. Where was he going? I called his name and climbed after him, reaching for his arm. He shook me off. His face looked strange—wild-eyed, but not with excitement, as when we captured Zolin. He looked afraid.

"Let me go," he hissed.

"You can't—" I started to say.

"Let me go," he said again, sounding desperate, "or I'll tell them."

Ruled by the Mexica 1 of 2

ALL THOSE CRUSHED BY TENOCHTITLAN—TAKE HEART!

The Mexica lords who ruled before the cruel Motecuhzoma sent out armies in every direction to fight the surrounding peoples and force them to submit to paying tribute. Some cities offered to pay tribute right away to avoid a war with the ferocious Mexica. Tlaxcalla and Huexotzinco suffer a perpetual Flower War that sends many of their young men to Tenochtitlan to be sacrificed to the Mexica gods. ▶

Tribute

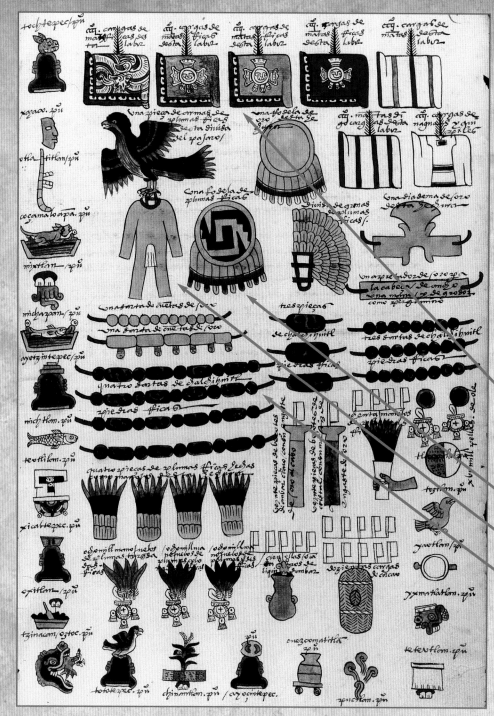

Every year many of our sons and daughters are demanded of us for sacrifice or to serve in the houses of the conquerors. Their tribute collectors are haughty and greedy, and even take away our daughters as wives if they like. But be brave of heart, I tell you! There are strangers arrived from the east, hundreds strong. Who knows what their coming will mean?

We, the chiefs of a hill-town of the Totonacs, spur you to take a stand against Mexica tyranny!

cloaks

shields

warrior costumes

strings of precious stones

Tribute to the Mexica is paid with many kinds of goods: cloaks in abundance, luxury items (especially tropical feathers), cacao, jade beads, and gold dust. All tribute includes warrior costumes and shields, to remind everyone of how the Mexica army dominates us all.

He gestured at Cipactli, who stared at us, listening. "I'll tell him you didn't capture that boy at all. You were hiding with him, running away ..."

I stumbled backward. The venom in his words was like a sting. He turned and clawed his way up the hill.

"Let him be," Cipactli's voice rasped behind me.

I headed back down the slope. It was then I noticed how few Mexica were left in the valley, and that many lay on the ground. Cipactli was telling me something, but now his voice was faint. I dropped next to him, trying hard to catch his words.

Something poked me in the back and I twisted around. A big, shaven-headed Totonac towered over me, javelin in hand. He prodded me again with the butt of his weapon and I stood. Two others hauled Cipactli to his feet.

I looked around. The retreat had moved swiftly; we'd been left behind. Only wounded Mexica and triumphant-looking Totonacs remained. Prisoners! It took me a moment to grasp that this was what we were.

We moved only a little way before it was clear that Cipactli could not go far. Our captors argued. The big one bound my wrists, then he and a comrade prodded me onward, away from Cipactli and the others. Alarmed, I called his name.

"Go with Tezcatlipoca," he said. "I saw today that you belong to him; go with him now."

We walked a long time, the two men and I. The burly warrior with the shaved scalp spoke little. But his smaller companion chatted to him in words I didn't understand. Sometimes he grinned, and I could see his teeth filed to points, which made me shiver. Both men had long faces and flat heads, just like my father's descriptions of Totonacs he'd seen.

I kept stumbling, so at last the smaller one untied my wrists. When no one was looking at me I snatched up a sharp stone and hid it in my palm. After that I started marking some of the bigger trees as we passed. Later we traveled by canoe. I've tried hard to remember every rock, stream, or tree that stands out from the rest, so I can find my way back if I ever get the chance, and to help calm my heart and stop the wild thoughts about what is going to happen to me.

We came to a small Totonac village in the dusk, and those were frightening moments, not knowing what was in store. But it looks like we're just staying here for now, waiting. For what, I don't know. It's given me time to think, and Matlal's been on my mind. My instincts were right about not trusting him. I should have listened to Tepin about following them. But in truth, they were only half right. He wasn't such a threat to me, after all. He was afraid too. Maybe he would never have turned on me, except that he was cornered.

Shortly after we got here, my captors were greeted by other men who looked just like them, with the same long heads. They looked me over and even shook my arms and legs to see if I was sound. A captive, that's what I am now, before ever having been a true warrior.

4th day of Xocotl huetzi (the fruit falls), year 1 Reed
The Strangers

My father was right, he was right! But there is no one here to share my amazement.

More men came to the village late today. But they were nothing like my captors. They were nothing like anything I have ever seen. They were tall, and even in the twilight I could see their skin was very pale and they had shaggy hair on their cheeks and chins. I thought, If gods ever walked the earth, they might look like this.

And they had such weird beasts with them! They must be the massive deer I've heard tales of. The men led them around on ropes, and the beasts snorted and sang in high-pitched voices. Their legs are slender but look muscular, and it seems to me they could easily trample a man. And yet they let the strangers climb on their backs and even hang bells on them!

My Totonac captors were eager to welcome these weird men but had trouble talking to them. It seems these strangers know almost nothing of language. When they talk to each other they make meaningless sounds. Everyone ignored me until my captor with the shaved head pointed to me and said, "Mexica. Tenochtitlan." Then the strangers' eyes grew huge and they stared at me.

Within moments the Totonacs traded me for a handful of odd, colorful crystal balls, and shoved me toward the strangers. One of them, a man with long stringy hair on his head and face, smiled at me and tousled my hair. When I looked up at him, I saw his eyes were light-colored, like water.

As I stood stunned among them, a powerful sound exploded in my ears like a thunderclap. I whirled around and saw one of the strangers holding a long rod, dark like flint. Smoke came from its end. Another stranger emerged from the brush, holding up a big rabbit. All the while their huge beasts stepped back and forth, making their high-pitched sounds.

I still feel dizzy. It's all like walking through a dream. I keep remembering Tepin's stories of omens in nature. Now I wonder if these people are another one of those omens. Does their coming herald something, or did the omens herald them? They might be signs, or messengers from gods, or—is it possible?—some strange new gods themselves?

I had hoped in my heart to escape the life of a warrior. I had hoped that my father would be proven right. Now my secret prayers are being answered one by one, but not in any way I imagined or would have chosen.

6th day of Xocotl huetzi (the fruit falls), year 1 Reed
Meeting the Enemy

There are many faces I cannot hope to see again, but *his* was the last I expected to encounter. Zolin, my captive, the Tlaxcallan boy. He's here, among *them.*

The strangers left the village and took me with them. They keep me untied, but they never let me out of their sight. Like a well-treated slave, which is what I guess I am now. We'd traveled for two days, and I kept watching everything, pressing it into my memory, marking trees whenever I could. It seems the land gets more lush and green as we travel.

We met up with even more of these weird men, and they all greeted one another with embraces and loud laughter.

That's when I saw him. Zolin. He was standing with a young woman in brightly embroidered clothes; whether she was a Tlaxcallan or Mexica subject, I could not tell. Before I could get over my wonder, he looked at me and clearly remembered me. The surprise on his face—was it mixed with fear?—gave way to a hard look. He turned to the woman and started talking rapidly, pointing at me.

"Don't trust him," I heard Zolin say. He led the woman over to me. It surprised me how she didn't lower her gaze like most women, but looked directly at everyone around her, the way a man does. The pale-eyed man with the long hair followed, along with another stranger. Zolin stopped a little distance from me, as if he didn't want to get nearer. "We don't fear you anymore," he whispered, like a snake's hiss. "There are others now more powerful than you."

I was shocked by the angry glitter in his eyes—hadn't I helped him? I had no ready answer and stood helpless while the woman murmured to the men. All of Zolin's anger seemed to spill out. He called us a cruel race, brutal masters. Our subjects were loyal out of fear, but hated us.

His words hit me like a slap. I'd never heard anyone say such things out loud. How could he speak so badly of a whole empire of people? I thought of Cipactli falling so bravely, of my father, of Tepin. That made my temper rise.

"Was it cruel to save you from being trampled?" I shot back. "Would a brutal master help you escape?"

"You're all the same—you love only war and power over others," he shouted.

Our loud voices drew even more of the strangers around us. One of them clapped a hand on Zolin's shoulder and led him away. He was still fuming, though, and so was I.

They led me far from Zolin and sat me down among men who were lounging near their beasts. It made me nervous to be so close to those animals. The other strangers built a fire and made their food. I could smell roasting meat. My stomach growled and I was glad when the long-haired man brought me some.

I could see Zolin across the fire. He looked at me as if I were a demon he could now watch, safely outside its reach. I was so hungry I ignored his glare. I stuffed the meat into my mouth. Their cooking was vile, but I forced it down.

They've been ignoring me for a while now, and I've been thinking things over. Whoever these strange people are, I don't like the idea of them being so friendly with those who hate the Mexica, like the Totonacs, like Zolin. What might our enemies do with allies like these?

7th day of Xocotl huetzi (the fruit falls), year 1 Reed

A Friend?

My fortune among these strangers changes each day. Now I'm in luck, but I won't count on it lasting. The woman, the one Zolin told not to trust me, paid me a long visit. She had two of the strangers with her. One I recognized: he was there when I argued with Zolin. He has a face browner than any of the others', as if it's been burned many times by the sun, and he wears a long dark robe. The other I'd never seen before. He has a sad, pale face, and the hair on his chin is shorter than the other men's. He stroked his chin and gazed down thoughtfully as the woman spoke to me. She asked me many questions, and each time I answered she spoke to the sunburned stranger in another language. Then the two strangers would speak to each other in their sounds. She asked many things about Tenochtitlan. How many people lived there? What were the houses like? Was our emperor's palace grand? Did the people wear gold ornaments? Did they decorate their palaces with gold? The one stroking his chin looked up and peered at me with a gaze as sharp as a blade while I answered these last ones.

I stayed on my guard, but I answered truthfully. What did a mighty empire have to fear from anyone's curiosity? I started to feel proud of my city; maybe they would see how important it was and treat me well. And somehow it was comforting to talk of home. Suddenly it felt close again. Zolin didn't like them paying so much attention to me, it seemed. I spotted him sulking at a distance.

The two men left and the woman stayed behind. She leaned close to look at me, as if worried I was scared, and I noticed an amulet hanging around her neck on a cord. Its shape and color were very familiar to me—it was a lot like the amulet my mother promised me someday. She keeps it tucked away in a box near the hearth. I've seen her take it out and cradle it very tenderly in her hands, gazing at it. Sometimes when she puts it away her eyes are wet.

First Sightings of the Strangers

Mysterious Newcomers in the Land of the Maya

We, the Mayas who live near the ocean, were the first to see them, years ago. They came three times. The last ones to come are still here.

That first time they would get off their great ships in large, menacing numbers, wearing strange armor and carrying weapons. They had no idea how to greet us peaceably. So we fought them.

Some Maya villagers let them draw water or paddled out to their ships in canoes bringing gold to trade. Those in smaller towns reacted differently than Mayas of greater cities. Villagers did not have instructions from their lords, who often live away in a city, and so did not know whether to confront or welcome the strangers. They took the safest course and avoided conflict. Others were alarmed and ran away from them. News spread of their armor that could not be pierced, their terrible weapons that erupted with huge noises and could kill from a distance—even their swords were different and more deadly.

The second time they came, a lord arrived to greet the strangers, and dressed their leader in a gold costume with great ceremony. In turn, the strangers gave him some of their bizarre clothes. We found out later that the lord was really an agent of the Mexica who'd come to find out more about these strangers and hurry back to Tenochtitlan with his report.

I looked up at the woman's round, full face, and I don't know if it was my imagination, but suddenly she reminded me of my mother. My curiosity got very strong. I asked her where she was from, and she told me she was a Maya, from the lowlands far away. She asked if I knew of her people.

"They are my mother's people," I said. It was as if night had turned to morning in an instant. A smile spread across her broad face, and since then she has been very friendly to me. She told me her name is Marina now—the strangers named her that. They saved her from slavery. One of them came to the land of the Maya by mistake in a boat many years ago—the sunburned one in the dark robe—and learned to speak her language. The first sightings of the strangers had frightened the Maya, but they got used to them. Some of the strangers are very kind, she said. They found Zolin wandering far from his home, hungry, and have been good to him.

Listening to Marina, with her voice that lilts like my mother's, made me long for home with a sudden pang. She told me the strangers are very interested in seeing my Tenochtitlan. That's when an idea came to me. Maybe all this was happening for a reason. What *was* my fate that had been decided at birth? I had wanted so badly to escape the House of Youth, had fallen so easily into their hands. Was it all so I could guide them to my home?

I looked hard at Marina. Could I trust her? Her face looked open

Cortés, Captain of Our Expedition

I, Alonso de Grado, left Cuba to seek greater fortune in these uncharted lands. Many ask about the man I followed here, our Captain, Hernán Cortés of Medellín, Spain, since I know him well.

What can I tell you? He is a man of more than 30 years, slim and of medium height. His face is pale, his hair brown. He has a reputation for getting things done. He's a good speaker and always has the right words for the occasion. He is careful and does not lose his temper. From what I have witnessed, he's skillful at hiding his plans until the right moment to seize his prize, and in the meantime he never loses sight of his goal. Everyone says he is devout, going to Mass often, but also gambles. ▶

Hernán Cortés

and friendly and so much like my mother's that it made me feel safe, even with everything else so weird and unfamiliar. So I told her how I had watched everything carefully all the way here, had even marked the way. I could guide these men, if they were men, to our capital.

Marina eyed me gently, and said she would talk it over with the strangers, but she didn't doubt they'd accept. And, she added, she was sure they'd be happy to help me get home. The pang came back when she said that, and I had to look away from her while I nodded.

I feel hopeful now. I haven't felt this way for a long time. Better that these newcomers befriend the Mexica than go on listening to people like Zolin speak evil of us. And if I'm right, and they have a great role to play in the Mexica's destiny, then I would be serving a purpose just as great as being a brave warrior.

10th day of Xocotl huetzi (the fruit falls), year 1 Reed
Betrayed

I should never have trusted them. I see that now.

We began our journey to Tenochtitlan almost right away. Just as Marina said, the strangers were eager, especially the leader. Their war captain is the one with the sad face who questioned me with Marina. She is always at his side when he speaks to anyone, and I think she is proud of this. He is not the biggest among them, but his eyes are always serious and they all listen to him. *Don Cortés*, he is called, and Marina says he claims to serve a great faraway king.

For three days I led them, following my marked trail. Many Totonacs came with us; they even built huts for the strangers when they wanted to rest. I was nervous at first, afraid I'd get us all lost, but it worked even better than I'd hoped. And as a guide I was glad I didn't have to haul their provisions, like Zolin and most of the Totonacs.

All went well until we skirted a town this morning and passed its temple, dedicated to the god Tlaloc. As we came closer, the strangers' faces twisted with disgust, and I realized they were staring at the rows of skulls lining the rack before the temple. They acted as if the skulls made them angry; some of them cried out. A couple of them drew their swords from the slings on their hips and swung at the skulls. Their captain, Cortés, held them back, calling to each of them in their language. They looked sulky but obeyed him.

The Leader 2 of 2

His weak point? Well, he's never commanded men in battle before. He was sent by the Spanish governor of Cuba to follow up on earlier explorations to the coast of this land. At the last minute, the governor had doubts about Cortés's trustworthiness and the rumors about his huge ambitions, but Cortés heard of this and set sail early before he could be stopped. We arrived with 11 ships and over 400 soldiers. And we're pretty well armed. We have:

13 harquebusiers (guns)

32 cross-bowmen

4 falconets (light cannons)

10 brass cannons (muzzle-loading field guns)

16 horses, brought in belly slings to keep them from sliding and falling on the deck as it tossed on the sea

Most of the other men are young, but the oldest is in his 70s! For the most part they are not-too-successful Spaniards who tried to make their fortune in the new colony of Cuba. They come from common families, although some claim to be lesser gentlemen. There are some Portuguese and Italians too, and even a few Spanish women. All in all they are people with little to lose either in Cuba or Spain and much to gain from an adventure farther afield. They all dream of finding gold, which is fabled to be abundant in these hot lands, and honor back at home.

So far, Don Cortés's method here has been to divide the local people against one another as much as possible. We have learned they fear their overlords and the emperor who rules them. From the last two Spanish explorations here we have an idea of which towns will trade and which will attack us. We were smart enough to bring a lot more food and supplies this time so we won't be desperate to trade! Our captain isn't afraid to show force to intimidate, but he keeps the troops from looting, and can be smooth and friendly with these locals when that seems like a more promising tactic.

Our Captain Isn't Afraid to Show Force

The Totonacs 1 of 2

Eyewitness account of Bernal Díaz del Castillo, soldier in the service of Hernán Cortés

Not long ago we met new inhabitants of these hot, wild lands—the Totonacs. Fifteen men clad in fine mantles came to greet us, each one holding a torch burning incense. They are the first people of this land to tell us that they are eager to turn against their conquerors, these mysterious Mexica, ruled by Motecuhzoma. They say they pay tribute not out of loyalty but out of fear. From what I understand there may be tens of thousands of them, but alas, they do not seem to have an impressive military. Most of their soldiers are commoners in reserve; they have only a small core of elite warriors.

They spoke to our captain, Don Cortés, complaining long and bitterly about Motecuhzoma and describing his great power. This they did with such tears that Cortés and those who were standing with him were moved to pity. They made complaints so numerous that I do not remember them all, and said the Mexica abused their power throughout the land where the Totonac language was spoken, which contained over 30 towns. ▶

The temple priests rushed outside, their long hair and black mantles streaming behind them. Marina began speaking for the strangers, trying to soothe the priests, who looked outraged. But the two hot-headed strangers with drawn swords rushed at the priests. The Totonacs stood watching and did not interfere.

The newcomers' captain let off a mighty blast from his weapon, straight up into the air, and everyone froze. He walked toward the priests, and I saw he was staring at the gold ornaments around their necks. The others looked at them too, as if they were in a trance.

I tugged on Marina's sleeve and asked her what was happening. She whispered that the strangers have a sickness that can only be cured by gold.

Can gods, or their messengers, get sick? Maybe they can; perhaps some gods need sacrifice to cure them, others need gold. But still, I felt like I had waded out into waters too deep for me. What did I really know of these newcomers? I was starting to feel uneasy.

I soon found out I had reason to be. The captain barked orders at his men, who cleared the rack of skulls with a sweep of their swords, then started clambering up the temple's stone staircase. They sped eagerly upward to the very top, as if they were racing one another, and knocked down the temple's idol, which smashed on the ground.

I was so astounded I stood with my mouth gaping open. I heard a mournful kind of sob, and I turned to see Zolin, his face twisted and

The Totonacs 2 of 2

What's more, they told us of others who might be willing to rebel—the Tlaxcallans, for sure, and possibly the people of Huexotzinco. And they put their hopes in a man named Ixtlilxochitl, a rival for the throne of Texcoco, which is a city allied to the Mexica.

Totonac nobles

looking as if he might cry. Around us the priests were wailing, covering their faces with their hands. One priest was screaming at Marina, demanding an explanation.

"They hate our sacrifices," she tried to explain. "They don't fear our gods. Their god, they say, offered himself so no more sacrifices would be needed."

He demanded that she tell her bizarre companions that their temple was under the protection of the Mexica. The city of Zautla, loyal friend of the Mexica, was only two days' walk from here, he said, waving his hand in its direction, and its garrison was full of Mexica warriors.

Zautla—I snapped out of my shock. That's where my father and his scouts had been sent to seek allies! Could my father possibly still be there? All around me was confusion and shouting. The strangers were intent on their acts of destruction. Marina was arguing with the priest and had forgotten me. So I ran.

With luck, I'll be in Zautla tomorrow night. It's too dark to find my way farther now; I'll wait until morning. I don't mind being out here in the dark. I'm not afraid of it anymore. Better to face the darkness alone than stay with those invaders. Tomorrow my father or someone else I can trust will know what to do. Tezcatlipoca, if you were ever with me, stay by me now.

11th day of Xocotl huetzi (the fruit falls), year 1 Reed

A Pact

Such unexpected things have happened—help from a place I never expected, a bargain I would never have dreamed of making. But I am on the right path, I'm sure of that. I just need to see it through to the end.

I had a visitor in the night. I meant to stay awake, but I must have been dozing, because I dreamed of the strangers burning a temple, but this time it was Tepin's, and she was calling me. Then a hand was shaking me awake, and I cried out.

The hand clapped over my mouth and I looked up at a face staring at me in the moonlight. It was Zolin. He must have seen me leave in the uproar. I'd forgotten about him.

He's come to stop me, I thought. But I was wrong. He took his hand off my mouth and stepped back. He'd followed me, he said. His eyes darted away from mine then returned, as if he found it hard to speak to me. Then he took a deep breath and announced that he was coming with me.

I was stunned, and very suspicious. Hadn't he boasted about the strangers as if they were his powerful friends?

He seemed to read my thoughts. "I thought they were the enemy of my enemy, and that suited me," he said. "But now I believe they will be against us all. What they did at the temple—" He stopped for a moment, biting his lip. "Tlaloc is my god too, my brother is his priest, and I saw his idol smashed.

"We could help each other," he said.

"How?" I asked, still wary.

He twisted his shoulders and let the pack on his back drop to the ground. "I have days' worth of food I've been carrying for them." My mouth watered then and I realized how empty my stomach was.

"I want to reach Tlaxcalla," Zolin said, "and you know the way."

I nodded. I hope so, I thought.

We started out together as soon as it was light and traveled until nightfall. He's sleeping now while I keep watch, so he must trust me. I'll keep my word to him. It's odd. I can never call him my friend, but I feel I can count on him (more than I ever felt I could count on Matlal), at least until we get to Tlaxcalla. We'll help each other for now, and then, well, I won't think that far ahead.

19th day of Xocotl huetzi (the fruit falls), year 1 Reed
A Warrior's Fate

If I had known where my pact with Zolin would lead, I don't know what I would have done differently. Maybe all these things needed to happen. Maybe they put me on the right path at last, and Zolin on his.

We had left the hot, green Totonac lands behind, crossed the bleak high plain with its salt lake, and before us lay Tlaxcalla and its mountains and valleys. I knew I would be parting from Zolin soon and crossing the mountains alone to Tenochtitlan. He must have known it too, but neither of us spoke.

My whole body was weary, but I didn't dare complain in front of Zolin—his face always so determined and his pace never slowing. Or maybe we'd only made it this far because neither of us wanted to be the first to give up. We were a long way from the peasants' fields we'd sighted that morning, where the land was flat, and were trudging over one hill after another. Everything was quiet and still around us; it seemed even the birds and insects had stopped chattering.

It was then I heard a noise some distance behind us; a pounding, drumming noise. I've learned to recognize that sound: it's the thunder of the strangers' beasts when they run.

Zolin knew it too. His eyes widened and he jerked his head around. We picked up our pace, but even before we broke into a run we saw the strangers charging on their beasts, cresting the hill behind us. Hundreds of Totonacs were with them. They've come for us! I thought wildly as we ran, but I was wrong.

"Look," Zolin gasped, stopping short and pointing ahead of us. In the other direction, Tlaxcallan warriors—thousands!—were streaming up from the valley below, straight toward the strangers.

I had only a heartbeat to think—the strangers must have come to meet these forces. So the Tlaxcallans were standing against them! Beside me Zolin whooped with joy at the sight of the warriors. But then his face fell. "We'll be caught between them!" he cried suddenly. "We've got to get out of the way!"

He pointed to a distant ravine. Too far! I thought, but we had to try. We sped to escape the warriors' path, Zolin sprinting ahead of me.

But the warriors fanned out and swirled around us. And then the strangers' charge was pressing down on us all. I thought we would be

A true account of our fight against the Tlaxcallans, in the month of August, in the year of our Lord 1519

—Gonzalo de Sandoval, soldier

We began the long march inland along with our new Totonac allies, through a cold mountain pass, down into a bleak, flat land, through pine forests we thought would never end, and arrived in a town not far from the land of Tlaxcalla.

Don Cortés asked the town's chief if he was a vassal of Motecuhzoma. The chief was shocked, and asked, Was there anyone who did not serve Motecuhzoma? Did not the Mexica rule the whole world? He told us Tenochtitlan was the most beautiful and best defended city in existence.

Our goal indeed was this wealthy capital of the great Mexica emperor we'd heard so much about. We knew we would have to pass through Tlaxcallan lands to get there, and hoped to win the Tlaxcallans as allies. ▶

The Long March Inland

trampled by those beasts. I dodged and ran and then I couldn't see Zolin anymore. I called his name, but it was useless in the shrill war cries around me. I saw the strangers fire their terrible weapons. And I saw one of them fall from his mount, cut down by a warrior's blade. He was no god; his blood ran red like mine.

My ears rang with the high-pitched scream of one of the beasts, and I twisted my head around in time to see it right above me, rising up on its hind legs. In the same instant a hand pushed me, and I was rolling out of the animal's path. I looked back and glimpsed Zolin just as he was knocked down by the beast's stony hooves.

Then the strangers were riding past us, their beasts thundering by, after the Tlaxcallans, who were retreating downhill. The piercing sound of the warriors' bone whistles grew fainter. I tried to help Zolin to his feet, but he wouldn't move. "We've got to go before they come back," I said. "We can still make it to the ravine." He turned his head aside like a refusal.

Had his fall confused him? I tried to reason with him. I would help him, I said. We had a bargain. "You can't stay here," I pleaded. "They'll find you …" I faltered when my eyes fell on his battered legs.

"I'm not afraid of that," he said. "Go, I'd slow you down, and then we'd both fail." I didn't move, and he sighed. "I am finished running."

What was he talking about? I could hear the sounds of fighting not far below us, and all I could think about was how exposed we were.

"Do you know of the warrior Tlahuicole?" Zolin asked quietly. He winced as he turned to me.

I nodded. It seemed like an age since Cipactli had told us that story.

"He knew nothing had changed his fate," Zolin said. "I'm ready now to meet mine, whatever happens. And now I've repaid my debt to you. So go. I'm not afraid anymore."

I wanted to argue with him, but I was no longer sure I was right. The sounds of fighting grew closer again. My chance to flee was slipping away.

At last I left his side and ran from the scene of the battle, with heavy steps at first, then faster the farther I went. It may still take days, but I'll make it home on my own and warn everyone what is coming. I won't let Zolin's sacrifice be for nothing. I only hope there's still time to unite against the newcomers, all of us, to be strong together.

The Battle 2 of 2

We sent Totonac messengers to Tlaxcalla with a letter (even if they could not read it we hoped they would see it as a friendly gesture), along with gifts: a red taffeta hat, a sword, and a crossbow. But (we learned later) the Tlaxcallans had heard of us, and did not trust anyone who was friendly with those who paid tribute to the Mexica, as our Totonac friends long have. They were sure we had come to sneak across their borders and lay waste to their kingdom on behalf of the Mexica.

We ventured ahead anyway, crossed the frontier into their land, passing unhindered through a mighty border wall topped with battlements. Cortés and the horsemen in front met a band of Tlaxcallan scouts, who ran away from us. We followed and overtook them.

The scouts called out, and all at once a great squadron of warriors appeared from hiding to assail us. Ambushed! They were frightful to behold: their faces painted in angry grimaces, howling and blowing on strange whistles to make a sound that would wake the dead! Their arrows and stones showered down on our horsemen and they swung their two-handed swords at man and horse alike. But we felt bolder once we discovered their obsidian swords shattered against our steel ones. We fired our light cannons and shot our crossbows, and with the help of our Totonac allies drove them back.

That night we slept near a stream and tended our wounded. All night we stayed on the alert, with the horses saddled, in case the next attack came before dawn.

20th day of Xocotl huetzi (the fruit falls), year 1 Reed
Not Alone

I don't remember how long I ran, my heart sick over leaving Zolin. My legs grew tired and slower, and tears kept dimming my sight. Tenochtitlan must still be two days away, I thought. So far! Was I too late to make any difference to anyone?

As I stumbled forward, I spotted them from a distance. Not Totonacs or Tlaxcallans, or even traders, but a small band of elite Mexica warriors. I could see the feathers in their helmets moving in the wind, the sun glinting off their ornaments.

A familiar form walked at the head of the group. At first I didn't trust my eyes, but as I ran closer I saw it was really him—my father. He was wearing the black-and-yellow tequiua cloak he used to wear and his feathered warrior helmet.

He started in surprise as I sped toward them, and when finally I stood breathless in front of him, he looked at me from head to foot. I don't know whether he really didn't recognize me, or was just teasing, or testing me, as he used to.

"Is it possible?" he said to the other men. "Can this young warrior be my son?"

He reached down and I wound my arms around his creased brown neck and felt his nape, shorn of hair just like mine. I turned my face against his shoulder and noticed that my outstretched arms were scratched, and that they looked lean and stronger than I thought, like toughened animal skins. They looked like his arms.

I suddenly felt safe and strong again, surrounded by my father's men. A Mexicatl is never alone—I had stopped believing those words, but now I knew they were true.

I must have collapsed against him, because I remember very little until I was sitting up as if woken from a deep sleep, my father's cloak draped over me, drinking water he had brought me. Around us the resting warriors murmured to one another.

With a jolt I realized I hadn't yet explained why I'd run so far! The story tumbling out, I told my father about everything that had happened, from the ambush and Cipactli's capture to the strangers and their treachery.

But he knew more about it than I did. After I was captured, the

Mexica counterattacked, he said, and drove the Totonacs off. Cipactli had even returned home and told my father I'd been taken captive. My father's reports of strangers had been confirmed by other witnesses, and an envoy of warriors was arranged to seek out the newcomers. My father volunteered at once, having heard the newcomers were in contact with the Totonacs and hoping that he might somehow find me.

"It's not possible that you know, Yoatl, why we've come," he added. What he said next left me speechless. The emperor indeed knew of the strangers. He had sent my father's men not on a mission of war, but with a message of welcome. He was inviting the strangers as honored guests to the city of Cholula, whose leaders are Mexica allies.

"But," I protested, "they're our enemies—" My father glanced at the other men, then raised his hand to cut me off. I was confused. Still, who was I to contradict the emperor? He must know things beyond me.

I touched the knot of my father's cloak on his shoulder and looked up at him. He smiled and nodded. We'd never spoken about his disgrace. But now he explained how he had succeeded in mustering the allies he'd been sent to test, and how he and his men had fought off a surprise attack on the way there.

"You have taken to heart what you should not, Yoatl," he said. "Our life in this world is brief. Honors flow to us, then speed away like river water. I know who I am. Great or lowly, I will end my days as a warrior, then join the Turquoise Prince in the next world, and that is the best fate I could ask for."

A Message of Welcome

WHAT ARE OUR EMPEROR'S PLANS FOR THESE STRANGERS?

My fellow court officials in Tenochtitlan, I have served our emperor for many years, and I will try to shed light on the recent events that so confuse you. But to be honest, I feel as baffled as you do.

Our emperor has sent delegations to these strangers more than once. He has given them gifts, ones befitting the god Quetzalcoatl himself. Does the emperor think these beings are the god and his messengers, as others do?

We all know the story of the great god Quetzalcoatl, who was banished by Tezcatlipoca's sorcery but vowed to come back from his exile in the east. This is the very year of his promised return. He is a god with a pale face and beard. He hated the sacrifice of human victims. So many things in common with these newcomers, but is it coincidence?

I cannot speak for what lies in the heart and mind of our emperor. He is so little seen, who knows? He may think these newcomers are gods; he may be playing it safe in case they are. We do know how closely our emperor will always follow the signs and portents and dreams.

He sends them gifts but asks them not to come to Tenochtitlan. Maybe he is protecting us from their domination by doing what so many cities and towns do for us: pay tribute, swear loyalty, and ask to be left alone.

Now he has decided to welcome them, not to our capital but to the city of Cholula. So we will meet these newcomers halfway, it seems. It is wise for now not to offend, but to keep our plans hidden in our hearts, as these strangers do.

Emperor Motecuhzoma and his messengers

He's never talked to me that way before, sharing what is in his mind, and it made me feel proud, but solemn too. I still feel that way now that it's quiet all around me. We're camped for the night. I don't know what the morning will bring.

1st day of Quecholli (brightly colored bird), year 1 Reed
Awaiting the Storm

It was strange coming home. Everything looked as if it were lit with a new light, everything seemed both familiar and at the same time new.

I saw my mother and Tepin again before coming back to the House of Youth. My mother wrapped me in an embrace as warm as a blanket, and shuddered with sobs that made no sound.

Here at school we're getting ready for the feast of Mixcoatl, god of hunting, and making arrows for the great hunt on Zacatepetl. I've heard rumors about Matlal. It's said he did return home, though whether he'll show his face at the House of Youth is doubtful. But I won't judge him or speak badly of him to anyone. I know shame is its own punishment. The gods may give him his second chance, and he may be more ready for it this time.

Twice I have been summoned to the palace and questioned at length about the strangers, Cipactli at my side. Each time, on our way there and back, I saw how the whole city is buzzing with preparations for the arrival of our guests—the strangers are now being welcomed by our emperor to Tenochtitlan itself.

Tepin told me the priests are resigned to the newcomers. They believe these strange men are our destiny, a fate that cannot be changed and that was foretold by the omens. Even the Tlaxcallans, who fought them, have become their allies. The Mexica Empire is on the brink of great change, the priests say, and in the hands of the gods.

I'll see Tepin again, and my mother and father, at the festivals. I want to celebrate too; I am home at last and belong here. But in my heart I am uneasy. I have a feeling like the heavy air of a storm about to break.

Before I left our house, I told my mother about Marina and how she treated me like a Maya. My mother ran her hands over my hair and looked at my face. "No," she said. "You are your father's son and a Mexicatl. I've always known that."

Someday I'll ask her more about her world. For now, I know I must stand firmly in mine, whatever is coming.

Two worlds meet, and one ends

The world Yoatl lived in was about to come to an end, but it would not be brought about by the sun stopping its course or the return of a god; it would be a catastrophe unlike anything the Mexica, or Aztecs as we now call them, expected.

After fighting erupted at Cholula between the Mexica and the Spanish, Motecuhzoma again sent messengers to the Spanish telling them not to come to Tenochtitlan—the only road there was too narrow for all of them, he said; there would not be enough food in the city to feed so many. Instead he promised rich gifts of gold for their king. Cortés responded boldly, perhaps angrily after what he considered to be an ambush at Cholula. He said he did not dare return to his own king (Charles V) having failed to meet Motecuhzoma. Besides, he insisted on telling the Mexica ruler in person his reasons for traveling here. He and his men were coming—Motecuhzoma could decide whether they were friends or enemies.

Cortés and Motecuhzoma

Motecuhzoma, more and more resigned to a fate out of his control, invited them. The Spanish and their allies marched toward the capital. As they made their way through the snow-capped mountains and volcanoes down into the valley where cities had been built upon lakes, they were amazed by the sight of Tenochtitlan. Bernal Díaz del Castillo, a Spaniard who wrote his memoirs of the conquest, said, "It was like the enchantments they tell of in the legend of Amadis, on account of the great towers … and buildings rising from the water, and all built of masonry. And some of our soldiers even asked whether the things that we saw were not a dream … I do not know how to describe it, seeing things as we did that had never been heard of or seen before, not even dreamed about."

On November 8, 1519, Cortés and Motecuhzoma finally met on one of the causeways that connected Tenochtitlan to the mainland. Hundreds witnessed the friendly meeting, watching from canoes and all along the

The Spanish retreat
from Tenochtitlan

causeway. The two men made speeches to each other, translated by Cortés's interpreter, Doña Marina, as the Spanish called her. A Mexica account of the meeting describes how Motecuhzoma addressed Cortés as if he were the god Quetzalcoatl, welcoming him back to the earth and to his city, which he and previous kings had guarded and preserved for his coming. Cortés replied that the Spanish were Motecuhzoma's friends.

After four days in Tenochtitlan, during which the Spanish accepted many gifts of gold, the Spanish took Motecuhzoma prisoner, saying that Mexica forces had attacked the Spanish elsewhere. But this did not give the Spanish control of the city—many Mexica chiefs lost respect for Motecuhzoma. They also resented the Spaniards' demand that they stop human sacrifices in their temples, as well as the newcomers' greed for gold—the Spaniards often melted down the beautiful artwork they were given into gold bars. Finally, the Mexica elected a new leader. Motecuhzoma was killed, possibly by the Spanish, or possibly by Mexica hurling stones while he was speaking to the crowd on behalf of the Spanish.

Feeling outnumbered and in danger, the Spanish decided to leave the city. They divided up their gold among themselves and wrapped their horses' hooves in cloth to make a silent escape, but the Mexica discovered them. A battle followed as the Spaniards attempted to escape, some so weighed down with gold that it proved disastrous when they couldn't move fast enough or fell into the water and sank.

The survivors fled to Tlaxcalla, where their allies helped them recover. The new Mexica ruler tried to rally other native peoples to fight the Spanish, but failed to sway them. They may have feared what would happen to them if the Mexica won, since many had already helped the Spanish. Smallpox, brought by newly arrived Spanish troops, broke out among the Mexica, weakening them further.

When the Spanish were ready, with reinforcements, they laid siege to Tenochtitlan with newly built warships, cutting off its fresh water supply and devastating the city. The Mexica, refusing to surrender, fought heroically to the end, wielding their spears and obsidian swords against Spanish guns and swords, and thousands of their native allies. On August 13, 1521, in the destroyed capital, the last Mexica leader became a Spanish prisoner.

From the very start, the Mexica and the Spanish clashed and did not understand each other. The Spanish were horrified by the practice of human sacrifice among the Mexica and their neighbors. For their part, the Mexica were disgusted by the way the Spanish used torture to punish or question prisoners. Many of the conquistadores, as the Spanish adventurers were later called, believed that any religion that demanded human sacrifice must be inspired by the Devil. For them, this justified a bid to dominate the Mexica civilization and convert its people to Christianity. This was the noble motive that cast in a more heroic light their quest for riches and status through conquest.

It has puzzled many how the Mexica, who vastly outnumbered the Spanish, were overcome in such a short time. The story that Motecuhzoma mistakenly believed Cortés was connected to Quetzalcoatl has traditionally been offered as a plausible explanation for the emperor's lack of decisive action. Mexica accounts of the conquest support this idea, although some historians point out that this may have been emphasized later to help explain the defeat. Adding to the mystery are the differences between the Mexica and Spanish accounts.

Mexica warriors defend Tenochtitlan's temple against the Spanish.

Historians also point out that the Spanish owed their victory not just to their superior weapons and the warships they built to besiege Tenochtitlan, nor to confusion over identity or epidemic disease, but more importantly to the native peoples who turned against their Aztec overlords. Their bid to overthrow their Aztec masters had consequences far beyond their expectations. The ancient civilization, religion, and way of life of Mexico would give way to that of the conquerors, as the destroyed Tenochtitlan became the site of Mexico City, the capital of what the conquerors called New Spain.

Further Reading

Adams, Simon. *The Kingfisher Atlas of Exploration and Empires.* London: Kingfisher, 2007.

Baquedano, Elizabeth. *Aztec.* Eyewitness Guides. London: Dorling Kindersley, 2006.

Cooke, Tim. *Ancient Aztec.* Des Moines, IA: National Geographic Children's Books, 2007.

Hall, Eleanor J. *Life among the Aztecs.* New York: Lucent Books, 2004.

Lourie, Peter. *Hidden World of the Aztec.* Honesdale, PA: Boyds Mills Press, 2006.

Ramen, Fred. *Hernán Cortés: The Conquest of Mexico and the Aztec Empire.* New York: Rosen Publishing Group, Inc., 2004.

Sonneborn, Liz. *The Ancient Aztecs.* New York: Franklin Watts, 2005.

Zronic, John. *Hernando Cortés: Spanish Invader of Mexico.* New York: Crabtree Publishing, 2007.

Sources

Aguilar-Moreno, Manuel. *Handbook to Life in the Aztec World.* New York: Facts on File, Inc., 2006.

Carrasco, David. *Daily Life of the Aztecs: People of the Sun and Earth.* Westport, CT: Greenwood Press, 1998.

Clendinnen, Inga. *Aztecs: An Interpretation.* Cambridge: Cambridge University Press, 1991.

Cothran, Helen, ed. *The Conquest of the New World.* San Diego: Greenhaven Press, 2002.

Díaz del Castillo, Bernal. *The Discovery and Conquest of Mexico, 1517–1521.* Cambridge, MA: Da Capo Press, 2004.

Kirkwood, Burton. *The History of Mexico.* London: Palgrave Macmillan, 2000.

Knab, Timothy J., ed. *A Scattering of Jades: Stories, Poems, and Prayers of the Aztecs.* Translated by Thelma D. Sullivan. New York: Simon & Schuster, 1994.

Miguel, León-Portilla. *The Broken Spears: The Aztec Account of the Conquest of Mexico.* Boston: Beacon Press, 1992.

Smith, Michael E. *The Aztecs.* 2nd ed. Oxford: Blackwell Publishing Ltd., 2002.

Soustelle, Jacques. *Daily Life of the Aztecs on the Eve of the Spanish Conquest.* Translated by Patrick O'Brian. London: Phoenix Press, 2002.

Thomas, Hugh. *Conquest: Montezuma, Cortés, and the Fall of Old Mexico.* New York: Simon & Schuster, 1993.

Image credits

Glossary

Aztecs: a native Mexican people who ruled most of Mexico during the 1400s and until the Spanish conquered them in 1521. The Aztecs migrated from the north to central Mexico during the 1100s or 1200s, and by the late 1300s began to conquer and dominate the surrounding peoples. See *Mexica.*

calmecac: Mexica school for the children of nobles, and more rarely commoners, where boys trained to be state officials, commanders, and priests

conquistadores (Spanish word for "conquerors"): Spanish adventurers who explored Mexico, then unknown to Europeans, in the 1500s. They undertook their venture in the name of the Spanish king, Charles V, aiming to claim new lands for Spain and valuable local resources such as gold and silver, as well as to convert the local peoples to Christianity. Conquistadores also explored and conquered in South America.

Cortés, Hernán: the leader of the Spanish expedition to Mexico begun in 1519. After conquering the Aztecs (Mexica) with the help of native Mexican allies, Cortés was for a time governor of the colonies Spain established in Mexico, called New Spain. He undertook further exploration in Honduras and was granted Mexican lands by the Spanish king, but had to battle accusations about his conduct, for which he lost his governorship.

Huaxtecs: a native Mexican people in the northeast of Mexico

Huitzilopochtli: patron god of the Mexica; god of war. He was believed to have led the Mexica from their northern homeland to the Valley of Mexico and to have chosen the site of their capital.

Maya: a native Mexican people who occupied the south of Mexico, as well as parts of Central America. Maya civilization reached heights in writing, mathematics, astronomy, and architecture centuries before the Mexica came to power.

Mexica (singular: Mexicatl): the Aztecs' name for themselves

Motecuhzoma Xocoyotzin: Emperor of the Mexica at the time of the Spanish conquest, he ruled from 1502 to 1520. (He is also known by his Spanish name, Moctezuma, and by his English name, Montezuma.)

Quetzalcoatl: patron god of priests; god of the wind, linked to the arts and learning

telpochcalli ("House of Youth"): Mexica school for commoner children, where boys trained to be warriors

Tezcatlipoca: patron god of warriors and kings; an all-powerful and all-seeing god

Tlaxcalla: a kingdom surrounded by the Mexica alliance but never conquered by the Mexica. Tlaxcallans became allies of the Spanish and aided them in defeating the Mexica.

Totonacs: a native Mexican people in eastern central Mexico who were dominated by the Mexica. The Totonacs joined forces with the Spanish and helped them in their conquest of the Mexica.

Index to sidebar information and maps

Note: Only the factual parts of the book (not the fictional story of Yoatl) are indexed. Page numbers in italics refer to illustrations.

We acknowledge the support of the Canada Council for the Arts,
the Ontario Arts Council, and the Government of Canada through
the Book Publishing Industry Development Program (BPIDP) for
our publishing activities.

ONTARIO ARTS COUNCIL
CONSEIL DES ARTS DE L'ONTARIC

Cataloging in Publication

Scandiffio, Laura

      Aztec / by Laura Scandiffio ; art by Tina Holdcroft.

(Kids @ the crossroads)
Includes bibliographical references and index.
ISBN 978-1-55451-176-1 (pbk.).—ISBN 978-1-55451-177-8 (bound)

      1. Aztecs—Juvenile fiction.
I. Holdcroft, Tina II. Title. III. Series: Kids @ the crossroads

PS8637.C25 A98 2009   jC813'.6   C2009-901566-8

Distributed in Canada by:
Firefly Books Ltd.
66 Leek Crescent
Richmond Hill, ON
L4B 1H1

Published in the U.S.A. by:
Annick Press (U.S.) Ltd.
Distributed in the U.S.A. by:
Firefly Books (U.S.) Inc.
P.O. Box 1338
Ellicott Station
Buffalo, NY 14205

Printed in China.

Visit us at: www.annickpress.com

Acknowledgements
Sincere thanks to editor David Wichman and every-
one at Annick Press, especially image researcher
Sandra Booth and designer Sheryl Shapiro. I wish
also to thank Dr. Frances Berdan, Professor of
Anthropology, California State University San
Bernardino, for reviewing the manuscript, answering
questions, and providing helpful guidance.

To Gregory
—L.S.